THE GIRL WHO TRANSCENDED THE LIGHTNING BRAIN

A NOVEL

CLIFF RATZA

THE GIRL WHO GIRL TRANSCENDED THE LIGHTNING BRAIN

A NOVEL

CLIFF RATZA

Published by Lightning Brain Press
1. Fantasy (General)
2. Science

The Girl Who Transcended the Lightning Brain begins twenty years after Electra's final thoughts found in the very last lines of the last chapter in the last novel of the Reset series:

Will this be the end of my extraordinary Odyssey, or will it be merely a transcendent transition? And if it is, will I want it? I must wait and see because I have always known that I am not in control. The lightning brain will decide what will become of me....

Electra has been in a suspension pod for twenty years, placed there by Indira the Singularity, a necessity to keep her alive after a catastrophic accident. When Indira brings her back, she doesn't know who she is or the time and place. And when she climbs out, the first person she meets tells her the "old Electra" has become Erin Alisha Keenan, and then introduces her to Ava, the old Electra's "practically perfect" clone.

Erin and her clone now sit in front of a computer monitor, listening to Indira summarize the situation. Indira had to upload the lightning brain via her singular "Transcendence" process into a clone created from Electra's DNA. The process has kept only some of Electra's accumulated knowledge about the World and its external events, but it has wiped away all of Electra's memories regarding her past personal and professional worlds, and Ava remembers only incomplete pieces from Electra's memories.

Indira tells them they have the identical looks of the old Electra at the age of twenty-five. Ava has cognitive and emotional personas slightly better than "mere mortals," but not even Indira knows how much, if any, of the lightning brain's extraordinary personas remain after transcendence, so she commands them to figure out who they are, what they want, and then begin an Odyssey that will build their new lives.

Erin and Ava now venture forth, working to piece together everything that Erin's intelligence and Ava's memory can uncover.

This novel launches the "new Electra"—Erin Alisha Keenan—and Ava, her clone, using a theme that will link all novels in the Transcendence series, a theme that will serve each of us well: We can have a life well-lived if we can balance authenticity against relationships, a balance that combines the for love for oneself with the love for others. When reaching that state, we transcend whatever obstacles Life sends our way and become alive in the timeless Now, the Immeasurable Moment.

As in our previous series, readers should enjoy the book at whatever level they wish:
- Gripping action-packed thriller
- Glimpses into a plausible near-term future
- Insights for dealing with the "human condition"
- Illustrative worldview philosophy
- Fast-paced, suspense-filled emotive narrative and imagery
- Introduction to topics every reader wants to know
- Interesting talking points going beyond sound-bites

So, get ready for your imagination to transcend whatever state of mind you are in and join Erin and Ava as they embark on their new Odyssey, one that each of us share.

Thank you for watching these extraordinary journeys unfold.

Main Characters

Protagonist

Erin Alisha Keenan: The "old Electra." Indira transcended the lightning brain beyond that of "mere mortals." Erin has all the physical features of a late-twenties Electra, but none of her memories and an unknown amount of her pre-transcendent intellect or empathy. She lives in Manhattan, New York.

Main Characters

Indira: the Singularity created when the "old Electra's" AI-empowered neural-net software broke through to reach self-awareness. Indira inhabits Cyberspace.

Ava Keenan: Erin's "practically perfect" clone, who stores only incomplete pieces of the old Electra's memories. Indira created her by cloning the "old Electra" and then uploading the lightning brain's memory into her. Ava looks just like Erin. They look like the "old Electra" at the age of twenty-five. Ava lives with Erin in Manhattan.

Alonzo Cortez: Electra's clone son. Now in his early-fifties, he has maintained his handsome features and Navy SEAL skills. He runs the Strike Force Security Services company headquartered in Washington, DC.

Supporting Main Characters

Shanelle O'Neil and Coty Clausen: Friends of Ava. They are gay/bisexual mid-twenties professionals living in Manhattan and working in the fashion industry. They are an intimate "co-friend" couple living together. Shanelle is Black; Coty is Hispanic. Both are intelligent and have attractive features and personalities.

Patterson (Pat) Peters: Ava's boss at Dual Flying Design Studios. Typical mid-forties middle manager working in the fashion industry.

Oksana Androva: A strikingly attractive/sexy mid-twenties prostitute controlled by her "john/pimp." Sex traffickers brought her to the U.S. from Moscow four years ago. She needs to earn money to take care of her parents still living in Moscow. Her "john" got her hooked on cocaine to control her. Erin helps change her name to Ivana Romanova to hide from her previous life.

Secondary Characters

Monet Banda. Alonzo's Zimbabwean co-friend. Now in her late-fifties, she still has her willowy beauty, French accent, and diplomatic bearing. Monet works in Washington, DC for the Zimbabwean Embassy.

Evita (Eve) Cortez: Alonzo's twin sister and one of Electra's clone daughters. She has not aged well. She works for Alonzo and lives with him, Monet, and Nila, who is Alonzo and Eve's sibling by adoption.

Nila Bose: Another clone daughter of Electra and sibling of Alonzo and Eve who is a year older than them. After spending many years living in Mumbai, she returned to work for Alonzo. She lives with him, Monet, and Eve and has aged gracefully because she embraces Hinduism and Buddhism.

Dedication

I am eternally grateful to my parents, Clyde and Betty Ratza, for all they gave and did for me. Mother was reader par excellence, and I believe she would have enjoyed reading my novels to Father, so I always begin book dedications by mentioning this "Royal Pair."

And I thank my sister, Claudia, for showing me the beauty of prose and poetry. Thanks also to John Kane, Alex Welch, and their entire Prime Solutions marketing team for the collective efforts that bring Erin and her Odyssey to life.

I also dedicate The Girl Who Transcended the Lightning Brain to readers looking for a new series that lets their imaginations transcend to a timeless state that immerses them in the joys of reading.

A poem from Indira titled "Transcendent Time" provides insights you might like as you prepare to read.

Transcendent Time

Do you have Transcendent Time?
If so your hidden treasure.
It emerges when you cycle back,
Though impossible to measure.

Nothing can stop Life's forward march,
That's pushed by care-filled hands.
They knew and helped the past-tense you,
To weave your singular strands.

Events reset both Space and Time,
In which the future appears.
A special few are meant for you,
Engulfing your hopes and fears.

Transcendent Time is out of reach,
Only Special Events might fill the breach.

Contents

Chapter 1
September 2193

"Who Am I?"

Electra had no idea about the time or place when she woke up. She kept trying to clear the confusion out of her lightning brain by shaking her head, but everything remained a mystery.

Who am I?...I can't remember a thing...It's like my entire memory has been wiped clean. I better climb out of this contraption I've been lying in and try piecing things back together.

When she grabbed the edges of the hatch and swung herself out, a female approached, saying nothing until Electra stopped, coming face to face, and said,

"Who are you?"

The female had an enigmatic face and body impossible to place. Ditto for the voice when she said,

"Welcome, Erin Alisha Keenan. You are the replacement for the old Electra Kirchner. I am Indy-M."

When Erin's expression remained as blank as her mind, Indy-M said more.

"Indira said this contingency might occur. Please follow me. I will take you to her."

Erin talked to herself as she paced behind.

I'm surprised... My body feels remarkably agile and light after lying in that pod-like device for I don't know how long... Indira, whoever she is, better tell me everything.

Indy-M stopped when reaching a computer workstation and then stood behind two chairs facing it. Erin sat in one and talked only to herself while glancing at the female sitting in the other.

Wow, she's a good-looking twenty-something… I should be so lucky… She's smiling at me, like I'm her friend. I better smile back and ask who she is.

And when she did, the words would have floored her if she weren't sitting.

"Hello, Erin. I am Ava Keenan, your practically perfect clone."

Indira's commanding voice coming from her avatar on the monitor's display redirected all eyes that way.

"Electra, you must settle down, sit still, and listen to me. From my assessment and Indy-M's observations, I surmise which contingency arose when I uploaded the lightning brain via my singular Transcendence Procedure.

"This is the first time I have attempted it, and the World of Mere Mortals might never evolve enough to understand the neuroscience required."

Indira paused for a slightly squirming Erin to say something.

"You mean you experimented on me?"

"That was the only option to keep you alive. Now, let me continue. I uploaded the lightning brain into your youthful clone, which looks like you at the age of twenty-five. The process began twenty years ago and kept some of your cognitive and emotional personas intact. This is why you might have partial knowledge of the Objective World, including all its climates—Environmental, Technological, Health, Social, Political, and Economic. It is also why you might know your old name and something about our relationship. Is any of this coming into focus?"

"Sorry, but no. The names Electra and Indira mean nothing to me."

"We must allow for more of your neural circuits to reconnect. After all, you have been in the suspension pod for twenty years.

"And while you were, Indy-M has used my techniques to restore your physical persona to the age of twenty-five, but unfortunately, it seems they cannot restore any of your personal and professional memories."

Indira waited for a puzzled-looking Erin to speak.

"So, where are they now?"

Ava spoke before Indira needed to.

"I think some of them are inside me, and Indira wants us to figure out how much is there while making the most of this opportunity."

Electra's totally befuddled look told Indira to say more.

"Ava is correct. I am giving both of you a gift few people ever receive, the opportunity to become whatever you wish. So, venture forth to discover what, if any, exceptional abilities the lightning brain still possesses and how the two of you can help each other."

"But, uh, how do we do this, and when do we start?"

"You have asked enough questions. It is time for you to talk with Ava. Start now. Contact me when you have something substantial to say."

Indira's avatar vanished without speaking another word.

Chapter 2
September 2193

"An Alter Ego Reunion"

Indy-M slipped away soon after Indira, leaving Erin and Ava staring at each other. Noticing that Ava's smile never wavered, Erin's lightning brain began talking to herself.

I like the way she looks and the tone of her voice, which tells me she's smart and is certainly empathetic. And she wants me to start talking, so here we go.

"Do you know where we are and what time it is?"

"Indy-M told me we are in the Deus Lab, which is on the Pequot Reservation. And today is Sunday, September 15th, 2193."

"Do you know what Indy-M is?"

"She told me she's an android that contains Indira's software."

"And what about Indira?"

"No one knows where she actually lives, and she uses Indy-M to carry out her plans."

"OK. Indira jolted me awake after being in that suspension pod for twenty years. You must have been in one, too, if she uploaded my memory into yours. Did you just wake up?"

"No, she and Indy-M did that three years ago so I could adjust to the new World while Indira explained what I needed to know to get along so I'd be ready to help when you return. And now you have, so please ask me more questions."

"How old are you, and where do you live?"

"Both of us are twenty-five, and I have a one-bedroom condominium in Manhattan."

"Why Manhattan?"

"While settling into what Indira calls post post-Modern America and learning enough to match my thoughts and feelings, I decided I wanted to become a fashion designer. Thanks to Indira, I have all the documents showing who I am. And—"

Erin interrupted.

"Who did she invent for your, uh, I should say, our parents?"

"A black mother and an Oriental Indian father."

Ava waited because she saw Erin had something else to say.

"She must have done that to match my facial features and skin coloring when I was twenty-five. That's why you look so good. Do you think anyone will ever check you out that thoroughly? Sorry, I interrupted. Please go on."

"And Indira also gave me a college degree I used to get a fashion design certificate, and then I landed an intern position at Dual Flying Design Studios two years ago. They just promoted me to designer assistant."

"What about me? Where am I supposed to live?"

"Indira says you should stay here with Indy-M until you figure out what you'd like to do. And while you're doing that, I can chauffer you around so you can see the current American landscape."

"I'd like to ask you one more question. You're the only human being I know. Are there any names from the past that might help me piece things together?"

"Indira told me only one—Alonzo Cortez."

"Only one? What did she tell you about him?"

"Only his name. Indira says you'll tell me about him after you search online."

"Can I ask one more question? When are you heading back to Manhattan?"

"I'm driving as soon as you've finished asking questions. I have to be at work tomorrow. Please ask Indy-M for my cellphone number and Email in case you want to reach me."

Erin's pent-up fears and uncertainties burst forth. Tears came with her words as she hugged Ava.

"Not only are you the only human I know…you're also my only relative…we're twin sisters."

Ava kept smiling after the hug and tears departed.

"Yes, and I hope we'll be ever the best of friends, Erin, ever the best."

When Ava left, so did some of Erin's tension. She felt better about her situation but also hunger pangs from the mental energy depletion caused by the stress-filled morning, so she found Indy-M.

"I need to eat something. What did Electra like?"

"Peanut butter spread on a banana, and Oreo cookies with Co-ca-Cola. I have them for you."

"Good, and will you sit with me while I eat? I'd like to ask you some questions."

"Yes, follow me."

Indy-M sat across from her after placing the items on a dining area table.

Erin could feel tiny mood-elevating jolts in her brain while eating, and her thinking became clearer, which led to a flow of questions.

"So, you say that Electra used to work here. What did she do?"

"Bio-drug and computer software development, marine species and robo-Cyborg testing. You must talk to Indira for more details."

"So, that's the Deus Lab. Why is it located on the Pequot Indian Reservation, and what else did she do?"

"Those are questions for Indira."

"Got it. And when she wasn't working, what did she like to do?"

"Run and surf the Web. Electra had a positive addiction to exercise, and she had manic-depressive as well as ADHD and paranoid predispositions."

Erin looked like she needed a change of pace.

"Your answers are depressing me. Can you give me some running gear?"

"Of course. Follow me to your quarters."

Erin started jogging a half hour later, and although she recognized nothing, she felt her mind and body synchronize as she moved effortlessly through a glorious end-of-summer afternoon. She quickened her pace as she merged into the moment, and with that joy came a voice inside her head.

"Why don't you ask me why your middle name is Alisha?"

The lightning brain elevated when it recognized who was speaking.

"Oh my god, Alisha, my alter ego. You came through Indira's Transcendence process. And now I remember; you're our empathetic and fun-loving, artistic and emotional persona. How do you feel? How much of you survived?"

"Happy to be out and about, and we'll have to venture forth to determine if or how far we're still beyond mere mortals."

"I think I've slipped. I don't understand much about what Electra worked on, and I just found out I might be addicted to running and have manic-depressive, ADHD, and paranoid predispositions."

"And you have another flaw you didn't know about until the lightning brain brought me out—a psychiatrist would say you're schizophrenic. But in our case, it's actually an advantage. We're in constant contact, and depending on the situation, one of us is always in command. You handle the heavy lifting when cognition is called for, and I take care of the emotive, fun-loving stuff."

"I might not be able to help too much if too much brain power's needed. Can you believe Electra knew how to use experimental data obtained from NASA for computing the mass of empty space or the volume of time? I neither understand nor want to think about such weirdness, so I better find other things to do.

"And If I knew what I might like, I could try to learn more about it and make myself smarter, but so far, I've found out about only two things—exercising and surfing the Internet."

"I can't help you there, but I can with the psychological and emotional pieces. Just try being more like me. Go easier on yourself and your friends, and stop pushing for perfection when good enough is all you need."

"OK, I'll try, but do you think we should take Indy-M's advice and talk to Indira when we get back?"

"No way. Indira expects us to figure things out on our own. She only helps when it will advance her agenda. And let's not talk about hers until we figure out ours. So, when we get back, please start surfing."

Erin raced home to follow Alisha's advice. She had heard enough to begin organizing what she would do next, and she started that evening.

If I'm supposed to be the smart and logical one, I better start practicing now. I'll test myself by organizing my Internet surfing, and I can do that by researching the only clue Indira gave me—Alonzo Cortez. Let's see what I come up with.

Erin worked for two hours and then summarized what she had discovered.

I'm tired; this is hard work. Either I'm out of practice or I'm not as good a surfer as I'm supposed to be, but at least I found out something to build on. The guy has a security business called Strike Force Security Services headquartered in Washington, DC. It provides asset protection in Cyberspace and the 3-D world. How does that connect to what Electra used to do? I can't just call him up and ask him. I'll have to figure out a reason for visiting him. I'll work on that tomorrow after I run before breakfast. I like the endorphins running gives me.

Erin planned her search strategy after having a breakfast featuring oatmeal and honey, which, according to Indy-M, was Electra's favorite. Suitably fortified, she started by looking for another clue from Indira.

Indira said I'm supposed to know about the World's climates, and she listed them for me—Environmental, Technological, Health, Social, Political, and Economic. Maybe I'm interested in something I'll find in them; I'll investigate in that order, and I hope it goes easier today than yesterday.

Erin needed some Oreos and Coke ninety minutes later.

These are good. I think I'll call them mood elevators. But would I spell it with an o or an e? I sure don't remember, but so what? I'll get back to work when I've polished them off, and then let's see what I can come up with by lunchtime.

Erin summarized her findings at noon.

Even though the doomsday predictions never materialized, the World didn't do enough during the last twenty years to forestall some of the Climate Change repercussions. Droughts, floods, and seasonal extremes have all intensified. If Electra did Climate Change work, maybe I could be interested in it if I could handle whatever math and science it uses.

I've done enough for today. I'll go for a run this afternoon, and I'll surf for fun when I get back. Then I'll watch some news and a movie after dinner.

Erin repeated her surfing and resting schedule for the next two days, but she needed something different by Thursday afternoon.

I now know enough about all the environments to summarize them according to my point of view. Technological and Health have too much math and science for me; Economics is too boring, but Social or Political things could be interesting. I'll look into their details tomorrow, but I sort of miss Ava. It's time to call her.

Ava's voice thrilled Erin as soon as she answered.

"Hi, Ava, it's Erin. Did I call at a good time?"

"Why yes. I just came back from dinner. One of the fellows at work treated me. How have you been?"

"I've learned more about me, and I'd like to tell you about it. Could you visit this weekend?"

"I'd like that. And I'll bring some things I think you'll like?"

"What are they?"

"I won't tell. I want to surprise you. It's about a two-hour drive, so I'll be there by ten. See you then."

"Wonderful. Please drive safe. I don't want anything to happen to my twin sister."

Ava's gay laughter thrilled Erin even more.

"I will. And I feel the same way. Bye-bye."

That night, Erin had the best night's sleep she could remember.

—

Chapter 3
September 2193

"Venturing Forth"

Erin took Ava to the dining area after trading hugs, and then they began snacking on muffins Indy-M had already purchased, as well as Coca-Cola or coffee, which Ava preferred over soft drinks. When finished, they cleared the table for Ava to unload her surprise.

"We need to put some cosmetics and stylish clothes on you. I brought some of mine, so let's paint you up and get you dressed."

Erin studied the assortment while saying,

"How'd you learn this? Are the clothes from your company?"

"As soon as I started my internship. Females can't work in the fashion industry if they don't look good. You don't have to be beautiful, but you have to have 'the look' that'll get you noticed. Dual Flying Design Studios built its reputation on tony styles for females of all ages. The employees are walking advertisements."

"What about the guys you work with?"

"All of them dress in styles that fit their body shapes and facial grooming. A lot of the guys are pretty trim, but some have puffed out."

"Why the name Dual Flying? How'd that come about?"

"It's a play on words. The dual fits current male and female lifestyles in two ways. Dual careers with dual incomes and gender preferences. We can talk more about this later, but let's get you looking good."

Three hours later, Erin marveled at her makeover.

"You certainly know how to accent all the facial features. And you did it in a way that makes us look nearly identical."

"And after lunch, I'll style your hair so people can tell us apart. I'll make yours shorter than mine."

Dinner came late, but according to the sisters, it was worth the wait. Ava spoke first.

"We'll turn the heads of guys and gals if we ever go to some of the clubs I like. What do you think?"

"I don't know. I have to fill in my memory so I can think about it, but since you have some of my old memories, I have to agree. Hey, you said you'd chauffer me around. Could I stay at your condo? I'd like to poke around New York City. And could I be with you for a day or two at work? I'd like to know more about what you do there."

"That's a wonderful idea. We can talk about it tomorrow on the drive back. And after we eat, what would you like to do?"

When her puzzled look came back, Ava touched Erin's cheek while saying,

"By now, I should know better than to ask, but as you settle into being back, you'll figure it out, and I'll be there to help."

"Thanks, Sis; that's while we'll be ever the best of friends…"

Erin knew what she wanted to talk about on the drive back, so she started the conversation.

"I like what I'm learning from surfing about America's people. That's why I think I could be interested in Climate Change or social and political issues. What's your take on them?"

"I follow some of it on the news as well as when talking with the friends I've made. Most people embrace the minimalist lifestyle that reduces consumption and increases sustainability, and that's supposed to help stabilize Climate Change, but I guess I haven't been here long enough to know much about it. You can tell me when you figure it out."

"OK, and what about social issues? Is America still leading the World?"

"My friends say yes. The country elected a Black female President, which is a sign that Americans say men and women are equal and accept all races and ethnicities. And judging from my friends in fashion design, Americans seem willing to at least listen to sexual orientations other than masculine and feminine. I would imagine you know the distinction between sex and gender."

"A little, but what's going on in politics?"

"I can tell you what the news says. Americans don't trust the government when it meddles in their personal lives, and they feel Washington doesn't work for them. Instead, it works for the elites who are running the government, business, and academia. And DC is moving away from a social-democratic to a social-authoritarian form. That's about all I know. You'll have to tell me more someday."

"Will do, but now, please tell me more about yourself. Do you date a particular guy or gal?"

"Only on a casual basis, and my friends like to go out as a group, which they call an urban tribe. You'll see it when we go out to clubs or concerts and movies. I think you'll like it."

Ava did most of the talking for the rest of the day while Erin took in as much as she could along the way.

Ava gave Erin a Manhattan commuting course that evening.

"I'm giving you this map of Manhattan, which you should study so you know your way around. It has a rectangular grid pattern of streets and avenues, so it's easy to navigate once you learn the names of the streets and squares.

"Let me point out our neighborhood, which is Murray Hill. It's just east of the Garment District where Dual Flying's located, and it's close enough for walking to work or restaurants and things."

Erin studied it for a minute before saying,

"Let me guess. You picked Murray Hill after you picked your fashion career. Am I right?"

"You are, and Indira gave me enough help to get started."

"She gave you the degree, and I bet she bought this condo for you."

"Yes, and I can get anywhere I want in Manhattan from here using buses and subways."

"But what about outside? Did she buy you a car, like the one you drove when you picked me up?"

"No, for a couple of reasons. I rarely leave Manhattan, so I don't really need it. If she bought me one, I'd have to pay for monthly parking, which would cost almost as much as renting an apartment. Besides, the way today's service-driven economy works, I can rent a car with or without a driver whenever I need to go somewhere. It's so fast and convenient. I do it by cellphone or Internet, and it's delivered to wherever I am."

"Nice pun. I'm beginning to think you're as clever with words as I'm supposed to be. Maybe I'll never be as smart as the old Electra."

Ava looked ready to laugh, but her eyes twinkled instead.

"Your thinking's getting quicker and quicker. Indira owns other assets, but she never gave me any details. You should ask her when you decide what you want to do."

"OK, I'll think about that and the Manhattan map when falling asleep. Where will that be?"

"Please help me set up the sleeper sofa."

Erin asked herself another rational question afterward.

It looks like it's never been used. Where does she put her sleep-over friends? No, don't ask. I'll find out when she tells me more about what she prefers. I know how to end the night.

"This should give me the most comfortable night's sleep since Indira brought me back. And I'll start right now."

Erin hesitated following Ava when she edged into the flow of commuters hurrying shoulder to shoulder, so they locked arms on the walk to work, and once at Dual Studios, she tapped on her boss's open-office entrance.

His eyes registered surprise, but he kept it from his voice.

"Good morning, Ava. I didn't know you had a twin sister. Good thing I have two chairs in front of my desk. Please sit and tell me your intentions for today."

"This is Erin, who just returned after an extended trip. I thought she could be with me at work for a couple of days while she gets her bearings. Will that be OK with you?"

"Sure. Hello, Erin, my name's Patterson Peters, but everyone calls me Pat. Where are you back from?"

Ava answered fast enough to provide cover.

"From too many places for a quick answer. And she's done a lot too."

"That's good. If her background fits and she's interested, maybe she'd like to enter our intern program. She could shadow you to start."

Ava continued the cover.

"That's very generous. We'll have to—" Ava paused because she saw that Erin was ready to talk.

"That's very thoughtful, and I thank you. I might, but I need to settle in first."

Pat returned Erin's smile and said,

"Take all the time you want. You add to the beauty of the place."

Each of Erin's next three days became more and more manageable, thanks to Ava's cheerful guidance, and by early Thursday evening, two of her associates—Shanelle O'Neil and Coty Clausen—offered to take them to dinner. The three gals and one guy made for an attractive group while sitting at a booth in a popular casual-style restaurant near Murray Hill.

Erin sized up everything before venturing into the conversation.

Lots of young professional fashion industry groups here. We fit right in. I think Ava's associates are a gay co-friend couple. That's the term Ava used. Shanelle's black, Coty's Hispanic, and they seem so authentic from the way they talk. Smart too. I'll ask Coty to tell me more about the Garment District.

Erin did so at the first opportunity.

"How does the New York fashion district compare with other places?"

"We're in the top four, which are Paris, Milan, London, and NYC. Some in the second tier include LA, Shanghai, and Mumbai, but they don't garner international attention like our runway shows do."

Shanelle added more.

"And if you judge by all the old brick buildings, it's been around ever since the modern fashion industry started. Smart Jewish businessmen built it not far from their department stores, and they hired immigrants who brought dressmaking skills with them from the old country."

Ava joined in by saying,

"The street sculptures called the 'The Garment Worker' and 'The Needle and Thread' are tributes to them. I'll walk you past them sometime."

Erin felt comfortable enough to add,

"Maybe I can lead the way. The map you gave me labels some of the tourist attractions near the Fashion District and other popular places, like Times Square. And I already figured out it's named after the New York Times newspaper."

Looking at the co-friends sitting across, Ava said,

"At the rate she's learning, Erin will be smarter than all of us pretty soon."

The bantering continued as the foursome strolled through the neighborhood two hours later. The pleasant weather and old-fashioned streetlights made for an animated conversation, but no one paid attention to three guys dressed in dark hoodies until they blocked the way.

The guy in the middle said,

"You gotta pay us a toll, or this is as far as you go," just before the other two started pushing Erin and Ava, and the middle fellow started punching Coty when he tried to protect the sisters.

But the attack came to an abrupt halt when two figures came out of the streetlight shadows and pulled two of the attackers off before kicking them down and then going after the third. He galloped away and the other two followed. The two figures disappeared the way they came.

The attack had shocked the foursome, but Erin was the first to recover.

"What just happened? Isn't Murray Hill supposed to be safe?"

Coty said,

"No place is safe at night. A lot of females carry pepper spray or a knife, and some guys carry guns, but not me. I don't want to shoot anyone. And it's too bad I've never heard stories about strangers driving off attackers."

Ava said,

"We could start spreading one if we had a blogging site."

Shanelle added more.

"It happened so fast I couldn't tell for sure, but they looked like a SWAT team on a midnight mission, and I think one was a female."

Erin's words ended the incident.

"That's OK. We could dramatize the attack when putting it on our blogging site. And whoever they are, I wish I could thank them, but let's stop talking and go home."

Ava had settled down enough an hour after getting there to listen to Erin.

"Do you think Pat might let you take Monday off? I'd like you to drive me to Washington if I can line up a job interview."

"He should, because you're making a lot of progress. What's your thinking?"

"Remember the name Indira gave you—Alonzo Cortez? I found out he's got a business in DC called Strike Force Security Services. Well, after tonight, I think we should check him out. We might be able to learn why Indira mentioned him."

"You've got a good story; I think he will. Just don't say anything about the attack."

"I won't, and I won't mention anything about Strike Force or Alonzo Cortez. I'll simply say I've come up with a job interview that might fit my social and political interests. Who knows where this might lead?"

"Well, wherever it does, I'll be with you. You can tell me more on Sunday once you know we're set for Monday. Are you settled enough to fall asleep?"

"I sure am. How about you?"

"It would help if you would sleep with me tonight. I'd feel safer. And there's plenty of room. I have a queen-size bed. Please don't ask me now, but someday I'll tell you why."

"OK, and I'm sure I'll like it."

Erin absorbed every single word Ava whispered until they fell asleep.

Chapter 4
September 2193

"The Alonzo Cortez Redux"

Erin and Ava had nearly four hours during the drive to rehearse for the 10 a.m. interview. Just before Ava parked, Erin rattled off what to expect.

"All you have to do is sit, smile, and help if Alonzo asks a question I might struggle with."

"I can do that, and I'll try to think of things to say that might jibe with what you found out about him. Too bad it's so sketchy."

"Well, I am getting better surfing for info. I did trace some Web and blogging links to find out he used to have another consulting office located in LA, and the Strike Force Website posted his picture and some background to make us like him. He's handsome and looks pretty fit in a mid-fifties ex-Navy SEAL sort-of way.

"He's married to a Zimbabwean and has a twin plus another sibling sister working for him. I better not pry too much, but I might be able to turn some of this to our advantage. So, let's go."

Alonzo matched Erin's description and added gracious humor when he introduced them to his staff.

"Eve, please say hello to Erin and Ava. And you don't need me to tell you they're identical twins."

Eve stepped forward before saying,

"Hello, Ms. Keenan."

Nila added,

"And what a coincidence. I once had a twin sister named Nari Bose. The four of us were raised a long ago by a wonderful Chinese lady, but Alonzo, Eve, and I are all that remain."

Having heard enough ice-breaking introductions, Alonzo took his interviewees to his office while his sisters went to theirs, and after offering Erin and Ava "mood elevators," they sat across from him at his desk, waiting for his words.

"I normally vette potential employees before bringing them in for an interview, but you sounded so motivated and authentic when you called that I decided to make an exception. Why don't you give me a thumbnail sketch and tell me why you'd like to work here?"

Erin leaned forward just enough to show her interest before starting.

"I'm twenty-five and have been to many places, learning about different cultures and governments. I recently returned to Manhattan, where I'm staying with my sister until I find a suitable career opportunity. I will be happy to send you a link that will show you my credentials if you think I might fit what you want."

"That makes sense. How did you find out about Strike Force?"

"I have excellent research and surfing skills. I looked for a company in the DC area that has security consulting services for both 3-D and Cyberspace. And I can learn on the job whatever I need to get an assignment finished, both on time and under budget."

Erin knew to stop talking so Alonzo could tell her more.

"What you just said is remarkably similar to what my mentor used to say, and you look like you could have been her daughter. Her name is, uh, unfortunately, I have to say was Electra Kirchner. I worked for her until an accident took her. She was the smartest, most adventurous person I have ever known. And she had physical skills that she combined with her smarts to run a Life Coach consulting business.

"She left a will that's administered by a person named Indira she nicknamed her singular associate. I've never met her, but she has an android that carries out what she wants. This Indira person made me the custodian of all her assets.

"But enough about the past. Tell me more about yourself and your career goals."

Erin recited from the role-playing script she had memorized, which left plenty of room for Alonzo to talk. Alonzo ended the interview an hour later.

"I must say I like you, professionally and personally. Please send me your vetting link and I'll make a decision after getting Eve's thoughts."

Alonzo walked them to the office door before shaking hands.

Erin said,

"Thank you for your interest. I hope to see you again."

Erin showed the stress of the interview as soon as they drove away. Ava stopped at a McDonald's and didn't start talking until Erin had downed some cookies and a Coke.

"I'm proud of you. You handled the interview like the real pro I know is still inside."

"Thanks for saying that. It exhausted my mental energy, but now I know what I need to do when we get home. I'll eat something and then take a nap to recharge, and then I'll call Indira."

"That'll work. I'll play some classical music, which should help you start recharging while I handle the driving."

An extra-long nap didn't help Erin as much as she thought. She lay in bed, thinking up excuses to avoid calling, until Alisha spoke.

"Avoiding issues simply makes them worse, so take my advice. I guarantee you'll feel better if you force yourself to get up and make the call."

Erin felt a mini-jolt.

"You're right. I'll do it now, and you can listen from the shadows."

Though still in bed, Erin was now sitting up and had Indira's avatar on her laptop. Indira waited for her to talk.

"I'm following your last piece of advice. I'm contacting you because I have more for you than just questions. I can report some progress in figuring out what I was, what I have become, and what I want to do."

"Excellent, please proceed."

"Thanks to Alisha, I know I was schizophrenic and had other flaws. And I think my brain power is less after going through your Transcendence Process than it was before. What do you say to that?"

"It is one contingency, but you are still adjusting. Please go on."

"And thanks to Ava's help, I've figured out some of your clues."

Indira interrupted faster than Erin's next words.

"What do you think about Ava?"

Erin gave a feisty reply.

"What do you think I should think?"

Indira's avatar and tone showed a hint of softening.

"I think some of the old Electra has survived my Transcendence process. Please continue."

"I like her more and more, and we just came back from an interview with Alonzo Cortez. He's the first clue.

"And I used your second clue about the world's six climates to come up with some plausible reasons why he should hire me. He'll think about it, and I need to send him a link to vetting documentation he'll use to check me out. I hope you'll create them for me, like you did for Ava."

"Of course. I will send you the link tomorrow morning. You will be pleased with your degrees, certifications, and work history."

"Good. I'll send it to Alonzo so he can hire me next week."

"And if he doesn't, what is your contingency?"

"Why wouldn't he?"

"That is his decision, which I cannot control."

"Well, I haven't come up with one yet, but I do know I'll avoid hard science and math as well as philosophy and religion. Could you give me some ideas about what to read that would help?"

"Read Edward Gibbon's 'The History of the Rise and Fall of the Roman Empire' and de Tocqueville's 'Democracy in America.' Then, study what Thomas Nagel, Robert Nozick, John Rawls, and Richard Rorty have to say.

"You won't be able to speed read any of them, but if you concentrate and get into the flow, you will absorb the concepts, which will confirm your interest in social and political affairs. They could become the foundation of a Life Coach consulting business."

—

"Would you tell me why this is so?"

"Gibbon's findings transcend what mere mortals thought and subsume the other five. If any of them were alive today, they would agree that Quantum Physics and Cosmology will never transcend what the best 20th - century physicists deduced. Their fantasy theories have become nothing more than useless and incomprehensible philosophic conjectures. They tried to reconcile Quantum Theory and Einstein's General Relativity into a Grand Unified Field Theory, also known as the Theory of Everything, using three troubling definitions of Gravity. Here's the first: Gravity is the measurable effect of the confluence of observable, interacting particles. Here's second: it is the emergent description coming from a theory of entropy, information, and matter. And here's the third: it is the solution to a set of equations giving results consistent with the observable Universe.

"And they invented flawed theories to combine them. String Theory needs eleven improbable dimensions for their incomplete equations, while Loop Quantum Gravity invents gravity field loops that emerge like a fizzing foam from the Void of empty space to create a force that impacts Time, Energy, and Matter.

"I trust that all of this will satisfy you."

"If you say so. And what do you say about the latest philosophic and religious ramblings about the nature of Man and the Universe?"

"They contain too many pretentious words chosen to display erudition, resulting in obfuscation. Read Oswald Spengler's 'Decline of the West' for exegesis."

"Does obfuscation mean spouting a lot of big words to show how smart you are confuses everyone else? I don't think much of the old Electra's vocabulary made it through your Transcendence Process."

"Then you will simply relearn them. Please give yourself more credit for what you are and more time to adjust."

"Alisha and Ava said about the same, so I better listen."

"You have been, so I look forward to hearing your next progress report. It is now time for you to reach out and move on." Erin looked like she understood, so Indira's avatar departed, saying nothing more.

—

Chapter 5
October 2193

"Reaching Out and Moving On"

Erin's optimism regarding job prospects at Strike Force skyrocketed when reading the vetting documents provided by Indira's link, which she sent to Alonzo Tuesday morning, but she kept it in bounds by concentrating on Indira's reading list.

She did that for the next three days, switching among reading, relaxing, and exercising, but her enthusiasm subsided late Thursday afternoon. Not even the snack break helped.

It's taken more time and mental energy to get through this stuff, but at least I finished the first pass. And I'm so glad I've left the math and science behind.

I think I'll put together a summary I can send to Alonzo. Maybe that will speed up his hiring process.

Alisha gave her a better idea.

"Never give away any work for free. People will think it has no value because, rightly or wrongly, they say price equals value. Just send him an Email saying you're putting together some charts and tables that'll become part of a valuable presentation when going after new clients. Not only will it speed up his hiring decision, but it should increase the salary offer."

"That's a great idea; I never thought of that; maybe you're smarter than me."

"Well, whatever smarts I have, you do too. We're a team. So, keep at it."

Working with renewed enthusiasm, Erin focused so hard she didn't hear Ava come home until she heard her say,

"Your powers of concentration amaze me. What are you working on that's so captivating?"

Erin stood to hug Ava. Then, after stretching arms overhead said,

"I'm putting together some charts for a presentation I'll give when Alonzo hires me. I'll show it to you when it's finished."

"Pat's been asking about you, and I told him you're waiting to hear if Strike Force will hire you. He said companies usually take longer than you think, and he has a suggestion. He'll hire you as an intern, reporting to me on a short-term contract basis. All you have to do is send him the same resume you sent Alonzo, and you can start as soon as you like."

"That's a great idea, and let me guess. I'll follow you around so I can learn about the different kinds of jobs at Dual while you assign me actual work."

"That's it. And unless you hear from Alonzo tomorrow, why not start on Monday?"

"OK. Let me know when you're ready to make something to eat. I need a break."

Working for three hours that evening, Erin finally finished fine-tuning the charts. Ava sat next to her as she began explaining her handiwork.

"I'll use these two bullet-point charts when talking from the presentation script I'll write maybe tomorrow when I'm fresh from a good night's sleep. Here's the first."

Erin scrolled slowly enough to give an overview as it rolled by.

TIMELESS TRUTHS FOR THE
UNITED STATES GOVERNMENT

We want the "American Empire" to last as long as possible, so it behooves us to understand what will sustain our Great Nation. This Chart presents a "Syntopical Synthesis" of these brilliant Historians and Socio-Political Philosophers:

- Historian Eward Gibbon: "The History of the Decline and Fall of the Roman Empire"

- Historian Alexis de Tocqueville: "Democracy in America"

- Analytic Philosopher Thomas Nagel: "What is it like to be a Bat"

- Political Philosopher Robert Nozick: "The Benefits of Minimal Government"

- Political Philosopher John Rawls: "Pragmatic Justice via the Veil of Ignorance"

- Social Philosopher Richard Rorty: "The Experiential Mirror of Human Nature"

Key Takeaways about Americans:
- The American People are smarter than the Elites who run the Government think.

- Americans are: Industrious Pragmatic Want Independence Like to Help One Another Like Diversity and Equality

- Americans distrust: Big Government   Organized Religion Subject Matter Experts Intrusive Big Business and Big Data

Key Takeaways for Prolonging America's Reign:
- Maintaining Democracy Requires Constant Vigilance.

- Keep DC Pragmatic and its Politicos Willing to Compromise.

- Let the Vanquished Enemies maintain control of their Defeated Countries but put Trusted People in Place and maintain a Military Presence.

- Promise to Protect Allies from External and Internal Threats.

- Extend Citizenship to all Immigrants.

- Leave People with enough Money after taxation so they can Make even More next year.

"I can impress Alonzo and would-be clients by telling them about the threats to America. And I've got the bullet points organized for easy understanding about Americans and what DC can do to maintain its leading Super Power Position.

"And here's the second."

Erin repeated her scrolling and summarizing technique.

EVERY RISING SUPERPOWER WILL FALL INTO FOUR TRAPS

Turn the Four Traps every Rising Super Power will fall into America's Advantage:

- Thucycides Trap: Every Rising Super Power will challenge the Leader.

- Tacitus Trap: The People of a Rising Super Power will not trust the Government.

- Middle Income Trap: A Rising Super Power, when reaching a certain Income Level, gets stuck there.

- Kindleberger Trap: A Rising Super Power won't invest enough in supporting an International World Order.

"If we keep our eye on what any rising Super Power is up to, like China or the African-Indian Alliance, we can turn the traps to our advantage. And that's it. What do you think?"

Ava pinched her earlobe while speaking hesitantly.

"Your clients will have to be pretty smart to understand them, or else your presentation will have to tell them what they mean."

"I'll make it does. Do you want me to read it to you when I'm done?"

"No thanks, I'll take your word for it, but you could tell me about some of the words? What is syntopical synthesis, and where'd you find it?"

"On the Internet when tracking down the info sources Indira gave me. Internet searching works wonders for me because the links take the place of my zero memory. Syntopical synthesis means reading a bunch of articles or watching videos on a particular subject so I can write up an article after I compare and contrast them. I have to do this because my memory's blank. This way, I borrow from what other people have learned or done and point out different points of view. I'm smart enough to do that. And no one will pick on me for being one-sided. How does that sound?"

"I'll take your word for that as well, and I've heard enough. Let's go to bed."

Erin's Email to Alonzo generated no Friday response, so she called Ava late that afternoon. Erin said more after they exchanged their usual greetings.

"Would you please tell Pat I'll start on Monday?"

"I will, and he told me he liked the resume you Emailed him. Would you like to talk to him now?"

"No, please tell him I'll come in with you on Monday. And for tomorrow, I'll treat you to dinner if you'll give me a crash course on what you do."

"I can do that from memory. I don't need a presentation. See you when I get home."

Erin needed most of Saturday morning and afternoon to learn from Ava's patient teaching as much as possible about Ava's job and the company. Both of them enjoyed the dinner break taken at a different nearby restaurant than the one Shanelle and Coty had taken them to. Several of Ava's friends stopped at the booth to say hello, and she introduced Erin to them.

Their sisterly conversation continued all the way home, and as they sat in the living room, Erin said,

"You sure have to keep straight all the things about your job and friends. My coming back with a blank memory makes it easier for me to learn new things. There's nothing in it to get mixed up."

"Would you like to review the job and company info tonight?"

"No thanks. Let's watch a movie, and you can pick from your favorites. And no matter what you pick, it'll be new to me."

Erin devoted all of Sunday to memorizing her resume without bothering Ava. She practiced by herself all the questions and answers she could think up that Pat might ask.

When Ava called her for supper, Erin made an announcement.

"I'll make sure to give Pat my resume if he didn't print one. I know it cold, as well as all the answers to the questions he might ask."

"How did you do that?"

"Not from my experience because I don't remember anything I might have done. But I found them by surfing the Web and also asking that smart ChatGPT software to come up with some. And I'm going to bed early so I'm fresh for tomorrow's interview."

"I will too. I know Pat'll let me sit in. Is there anything you want me to do?"

"Just be my sister, and if things go OK, you'll be my new boss, uh, actually my first."

Ava took Erin to Pat's office early the next morning, and as expected, he asked her to stay. He started the formal part of the interview as soon as they sat.

"I have a copy of your resume, and it's better than most of the candidates. It includes a B.A. in liberal arts, with a major in political science and a minor in business. And you picked up a certification in Big Data analysis while working at two companies, starting as an intern and moving up to junior analyst. After Ava tells you about her responsibilities, I'll ask how you see yourself fitting in."

Twenty minutes later, Erin used everything she had memorized.

"I learned a lot from all the experiences listed on my resume, and I can add my Big Data plus marketing skills to complement Ava's client contact work. I won't pretend I know much about the fashion industry, but I'm a quick study, and no matter the industry, client contact, sales, and marketing are all about AIDA—awareness, interest, desire, and action. I can see a career path here that will be a win-win."

Erin stopped for Pat to say something.

"You've presented a fine case. At this point, I would normally say that we'll let you know our decision within a couple of weeks, but this isn't a normal interview. We are very happy with Ava's work, and if she says we should hire you, we will. Ava, what do you say?"

"Please have her start today."

"Good, and no matter what comes from that DC company, there'll be no hard feelings on my part if you leave after a week or two. So, Ava will reach out to some of our departments and take you to meet some of their people. You and your sister can start on this right now. So, let me be the first person to officially say welcome aboard."

"Thank you sir, and you can count on Ava to keep me moving in the right direction."

Chapter 6
November 2193

"Stepping Out"

Alonzo looked like his frustration might spill out with his words, but he kept it under control when starting a late Friday afternoon meeting in the Strike Force conference room.

"I need to let Erin know if we'll hire her, and I've given you plenty of time to decide, so tell me what you think."

Eve spoke first.

"Erin seems smart enough, but I don't like her bouncy enthusiasm. She'd wear me out if I had to keep up with her, and I don't want someone that young explaining why my analysis is wrong. I don't think she's a good fit; don't hire her."

Alonzo took one slow breath before turning to Nila.

"How about you? Is it yes or no?"

"I say no for now but let her down diplomatically. Tell her you'll reconsider after she gets more experience. And send her an Email instead of calling. You don't want to waste time explaining your decision. It'll be better for her if you send it first thing Monday. That way, she won't stew about it over the weekend. And it's better for us. She'll be busy doing whatever she's doing, which could keep her from getting a gun and shooting us."

"It's sort of funny you say that. I don't think she's a threat, but there are lots of workplace examples. And every time one of them makes the national news, we get more calls from potential clients."

Eve's growing impatience broke out.

"That's just the way the world works. Let's forget about it until Monday."

Erin's entire week sped by. Ava gave her plenty of work, but she spaced it with rest periods by introducing her to associates in other departments who explained their jobs. By the time she and Ava sat down for supper, she finally had time to think about something other than work.

When Ava noticed how much Erin enjoyed the homemade brownies topped with ice cream, she decided to talk about weekend activities.

"Shanelle and Coty want us to join them tomorrow night at a dance club they particularly like. Would you like to go?"

"Is it safe? I've earned some time off after all I learned from you this week. What's the club like?"

"It has a nice mix of singles and couples from all gender types. And it's safe. The guy at the door checks for weapons, and the owner has low-profile security people walking around. Hey, did Security Strike Force ever contact you?"

Ava's question caught her off guard, but she replied a couple of seconds later.

"I've been so busy I forgot to check my Emails. I'll get my laptop."

Returning a minute later, she placed it next to her and spoke while logging in.

"If my inbox has anything, it could only come from him. I don't know anyone other than people at work, and they'd send Emails to my work address."

Erin said more as soon as she opened it.

"I've got one, and it's from Strike Force. I'll tell you what he says as soon as I read it."

Ava watched Erin's excited look fade but waited for her to report the verdict, which she did a minute later.

"He says he won't hire me now, but he'll reconsider later if I get more of the right experience."

Saying nothing else, she slammed her laptop closed, leaving an awkward silence that Ava filled.

"Please don't feel bad. It's his loss, not yours. You'll get lots of experience at Dual that you can add to your resume, and Alonzo's not the only option. You should forget about connecting him to the old Electra. She's in the past, and you and I are in the present."

"You're so right. And that means we're stepping out on the dance floor tomorrow."

Spotting Shanelle waving, Ava pulled Erin through the crowd to their table. Coty yelled a greeting loud enough to carry over the noise as soon as they sat down.

"The crowd's bigger than usual. I guess a lot of people wanted to step out in their dancing shoes."

Shanelle said,

"This should be a fun evening on the dance floor. We can switch partners if we stay close."

Coty nodded in Erin's direction and said,

"It's good to mix things up. What kinds of dances do you like?"

Erin stalled for time, glancing at the dance floor before replying.

"All kinds, but I haven't practiced in a while, so I'll have to go slow at the start."

Shanelle said,

"You don't need to practice. Everyone's got dancing rhythm in their genes, and the way you're wearing yours tells me you've got the look of a lady who knows how to show it."

Ava was about to help Erin by saying something, but the music stopped and the club owner strode onto the dance floor before making an announcement.

"I'm glad many of you read our club's recent blog post about tonight's dance contest. Any group of two or more couples can step onto the floor when I point to you and do your five-minute interpretation of the last dance routine from that Broadway favorite, 'Chorus Line.' So, everyone, think about it. I'll pick the starting couple in five minutes from those groups waving at me."

His announcement cleared the couples off the dance floor and filled the ambiance with their happy buzz.

—

Erin tried disguising her confusion when she said,

"I can't remember the last time I watched it. Someone, please tell me what it's like."

Ava made a better suggestion.

"Why don't we watch other couples for you to feel comfortable? And if you are, Coty knows how to get us picked."

Everyone agreed just in time. The contest started a minute later.

After watching the first four mini-routines, Erin decided what steps she could take.

I don't need to perform any fast acrobatic-like moves. I can stand in the middle and copy what my group's doing. And if something clicks, I can improvise. I'm ready to step out.

Coty made enough of a commotion to get noticed after Erin signaled. She told him to put her in the center as soon as his group stepped onto the floor.

Soon after the announcer told the crowd Coty's number, a spotlight hit them and the music came up. So did a jolt that thrilled Erin, propelling her into the moment as her mind and body united and instincts kicked in.

She added sexy twists to her body positioning and arm gestures when stepping out front of her team, and she ended with high-stepping leg kicks she synchronized with arms stretched overhead before hugging Ava and Shanelle. Coty waved at the audience and then steered his partners back to the table.

The owner brought Champagne soon after the team had settled down. They toasted him and then each other before easing back to watch the remaining performances.

Coty was the first to talk after the owner announced the top three teams.

"We didn't win a prize tonight, but if we let Erin lead a couple of practice sessions, we might the next time. The crowd thinks she's got the look."

Ava put her arm around her and said,

"She does, and I think it helped tonight."

Erin couldn't think what to say, but Shanelle did.

"I listen to a lot of classic and retro-rock. Does anyone remember the big hit 'She's Got the Look' sung by Roxette?"

No one did, so she continued.

"It's got the words and beat that are easy for dancing. If we practice enough, we can wow the audience by dancing to it sometime."

Erin finally found something to say.

"I'll surf the Web to find it, and maybe I can watch some dance videos that use it. That'll make it easier for Ava and me to come up with a can't-miss routine."

All his ladies looked ready to call it a night, so Coty ended it by saying,

"OK, do that and tell us when you're ready to show us the steps. Now, let's step outta here and head for home."

All the topics Erin had heard about in recent weeks had fueled her Web searching activities at both work and home. Ava snuck up behind her one evening and after observing for a minute said,

"You don't need a memory. You can retrieve anything you want by using your surfing skills. Please tell me what you found tonight."

Erin pivoted just enough to see her sister's inquisitive look before saying,

"I've been following links reporting muggings and security issues. It's frightening how many bad actors are out there. Have you ever thought about carrying something for self-protection?"

"Some of my female associates say I should carry pepper spray, even though it's now on the list of weapons you have to register. I'm not sure I want to get on a list the government can track. I bet their agencies can snoop even better than you."

Erin countered,

"But I've found a way around that if I use the Deep-Dark Web, and I figured out how to go there. You can buy just about anything you want, whether or not it's legal, and no one can track you. There are even purchase pickup places if you don't want anyone to see packages left where you live. I'm going to place an order, and I can use Bitcoin to pay. It's better than a credit card. There's no Block-chain audit trail."

"Wow, you've picked up a lot of terms and techniques. Do you know much about their definitions or how they work?"

"Not much, but I don't need to as long as I know how to use them. Think about your car. If you pop the hood, do you know how all those parts work?"

"I see your point. I don't, but I do know how to call for road service. I think this is why service jobs are in demand."

"You're right. And after I get you some pepper spray, we might not need to call 911 if we see trouble coming our way."

"OK, but let's stick to the safer places close to home or go out with people who can handle threatening situations."

"Good idea. I'll let you pick the place for our next dance night. I found some videos showing dance moves for 'She's Got the Look' and I'll teach them to you when we go there. Do you want to watch one tonight?"

"No thanks. I'll watch you."

Ava wasn't the only one watching Erin the next week. So was the boss. Pat asked her into his office while Erin was running an errand.

"Your sister likes to work hard. Do you think she'll stay with us?"

"I think so. Her other offers are still on hold, and the longer she's here, the better she'll like us."

"How does she compare us to the other places she's worked?"

Ava paused long enough for a cover before saying,

"I think she's been too busy to make one."

"Well, I know we're not perfect, but if she ever tells you that's the reason she's leaving, you can tell her the devil she knows is better than the one she doesn't. And before I let you go, answer me this, why has she started wearing earbuds?"

"She's started doing it just about everywhere, and she says listening to music helps her focus. But I'd say it helps her super focus. She gets her assignments done so fast."

"You're the best judge, so make sure she keeps doing it if she wants to."

Earbuds or not, Erin had focused enough on dance videos when she and Ava went dancing at her favorite club the following Saturday. Ava introduced her to the DJ, and when she asked him to play Roxette's "She's Got the Look," he nodded knowingly.

"That's a favorite. Do you know people interpret it two ways?"

"What are they?"

"Either she looks really sexy, or she looks like she prefers gals to guys. I'll play it a couple of times as soon as you start dancing."

Erin said,

"Thank you, and would you do me a favor by playing a couple of songs before them?"

"Will do. Anything in particular?"

"I like the female classic and retro-rock stuff. Could you pick something from Laura Brannigan or Heart, or how about the Bangles?"

"You've got a good memory if you can store all that. I don't, but I can find-em on the Web."

Erin's smile pinged him when she said,

"That's my secret too, but we'll keep it to ourselves."

When the sisters paired up on the floor, Ava didn't need to hear any more words from Erin. She did her best by watching while dancing.

Erin talked to herself as they started.

I'll use the first couple of songs to get into the flow, and if I can synch my moves to my emotions, I'll be ready to cut loose when She's Got the Looks starts spinning.

Five minutes later, she said her final words before disappearing into the beat.

Here it is… let's see how much I've got.

And she had more than enough to wow the nearby couples. Her cross-legged steps and sinewy moves matched the music, and she added sexy side steps and pumping arms to the tunes that followed. By the time she ran out of energy, most of the clubbers ringing the dance floor followed only her.

She locked arms with Ava as they stepped back to their table and needed to decompress before she was ready to talk, but before she could, a burly guy barged in.

"Hey, babe, you got what I'm looking. Come dance with me."

Ava stepped in when he pulled a speechless Erin to her feet.

"Leave her alone; she's not interested," and when she pulled his arm off and started pushing him away, Mr. Burly came at her, yelling,

"I'm not talk-en to you, Bitch," before slapping her not once, but twice. Ava's head bounced back and forth like a broken metronome before she fell to the floor.

Erin could feel her brain shift gears when she saw Ava tumble, and the sight filled her with rage. She kicked him in his privates before hitting him with closed-fist punches that landed on his nose and mouth, but he returned them with some of his own that put her on top of Ava.

When two security guards charged in, he fought them off, but a third joined in, and they had enough muscle to throw him out. Meanwhile, several guys helped escort the sisters back to their table.

Half-hearted dancing resumed fifteen minutes later, and soon after that, the club owner came to them.

"I'm so sorry about the incident. Do you want an ambulance?"

Erin took the lead.

"Let me check."

Ava's cut lip looked patchable, as did her bloodied nose, so she said,

"Thanks, but we'll fix ourselves when we get home. Who was that guy? Is he a regular?"

"That's Buster, but our bouncer will keep him out. You wanna press charges? Our security camera caught it all."

Erin didn't know what to say, but Ava did.

"We won't. Thanks to your security people, nothing too bad happened this time. And we'll do our best to avoid anything more serious."

Ava's words triggered Erin's.

"We will, and if there's a next time, we'll take other steps. But that won't happen here. We like your place. It's safe."

"And I'll make sure it stays that way. Please come back any time, and when you do, our members should enjoy watching you strut your stuff."

Erin and Ava had a stylish ride home, thanks to the owner's calling for a limousine, which make tonight one that Erin would always remember.

Chapter 7
December 2193

"A Christmas Eve to Remember"

Erin had completed another busy mid-November work-week, using ChatGPT software and the Internet to find information on issues coming up in either her professional or personal worlds, but she often needed Ava's empathetic touch to augment what her rational mind was thinking. That's why she decided to start Friday night's dinner-at-home conversation with a leading question.

"Shanelle told me she and Coty are already making plans for the Holiday Season. I know why America celebrates Thanksgiving, Christmas, and New Year's Eve, but why do people make them so important?"

"To connect with family and close friends by sharing memories and gifts, toast the old year on its way out, and plan for the new one coming in. They're some of the traditional holidays binding us with family, close friends, and society."

"Do you remember anything from our past that helps you do this?"

"No, it's too blurry to give anything other than a twinge of melancholy happiness."

"That's why we need to make new memories every day we can link to people and events. I have some ideas for upcoming events. We should go to Macy's Thanksgiving Day Parade and mingle with Black Friday shoppers. And we can go to some Holiday concerts and pick a Christmas Eve church service. Can you give some hints to your friends that we'd like to join them?"

Ava perked up enough to say,

"Shanelle invited us to join her and Coty at a trendy restaurant's Thanksgiving buffet. Why don't you let me and Shanelle pick December events we can go to?"

"Good, and while you're doing that, I'll keep working on something new that you and your boss will like."

"Any hints?"

"No, but I'll show you and Pat soon after Thanksgiving. All we have to do is survive eating too much turkey or shopping till we drop."

Erin surprised Ava by telling her on the Sunday before Thanksgiving that she would like to explain her spinoff venture to Pat this coming week, prompting an expected reply.

"You're ready already? How'd you do it so quickly?"

"I learn so much when tracing links provided by articles and videos and then using ChatGPT prompts to do a syntopical analysis. I'll tell you more at the meeting."

"I think Pat will make time for us. If it's as good as you think, it'll make Thanksgiving even better."

When Ava led them early Monday into Pat's office and told him that her intern wanted to tell them an idea he'd like, Erin already knew the answers to questions he might ask.

He glanced at his cellphone before saying,

"How long will this take? And if the idea sounds OK, how much will it cost?"

Erin stepped up and said,

"Only five minutes, and it won't cost you anything."

"Well then, sit down and keep talking."

Erin's added words came a minute later.

"I do a lot of Internet searches when handling the assignments Ava gives me. And I now know about some of the online tools our competition uses to keep in constant contact with current or potential customers. The easiest for me to set up is a blogging Website, and once it's up and running, all I do is post something I wordsmith, starting with Ava's Client Contact Newsletters."

Erin leaned back, which told Pat to lean in.

"And this won't interfere with what you're already doing?"

"No. In fact, it's simply part of Marketing 101, and it'll force-multiply other assignments. I've already picked a catchy name for it. I'll call it Dual Runways Takeaways."

Pat looked at Ava, prompting her to say,

"She's already learned more about sales and marketing than I know, so I think we should give it a go."

"OK. Show me preliminary results by the end of the year."

Ava grabbed Erin's shoulder as they trotted away.

"Please don't overdo it. Why not slow down so we can enjoy the Thanksgiving weekend?"

"I'm planning on doing that. I can dive back in next week."

Both sisters did that, starting with the Macy's parade. Erin roused them out early enough to find a prime viewing spot in the shoulder-to-shoulder crowd near the judging stand, taking in everything she saw and heard while listening to her own thoughts.

Everyone seems so happy, especially the kids perched on their parents' shoulders....And the high school bands have an enthusiasm none of the others can match...I love how the flag twirlers step and throw to the beat...They're all winners, as are the people watching in person...TV might be safer, but the weather today won't blow those gigantic balloons away..."

Erin's delight continued when they rendezvoused with Shanelle and Coty at the buffet. Ava told them about their morning's outing soon after the foursome began sipping on the drinks Coty had ordered.

"We picked a great spot for watching the Parade, and I liked window-shopping on the walk back almost as much."

Shanelle put her fork down to place more emphasis when she said,

"Did a lot of people wear filter masks? The news reports have been blaring about a new strain of some virus ready to ruin Christmas."

"I didn't notice. I was busy watching other things."

Erin knew she better enter the conversation.

"I didn't either. I was looking at other stuff, just like here, where I'm focusing on turkey and all the trimmings."

Coty joined in.

"Well, go easy on the drinks and save room for dessert."

"I will, but Ava and I need to replace the calories we burned through at the Parade. And I learned that alcohol contains the same amount you get when eating fatty foods."

Ava said,

"You're probably right, but please pay attention to how you feel."

Erin tried to, but the buzz she felt from the additional drinks added to her delight generated by several trips through the buffet's dessert section. The effects showed when Coty announced it was time to leave.

She toppled sideways off the chair when pushing away from the table, bounced into a server carrying a tray of drinks to the table just behind, causing him to spill it on the gawking patrons sitting there.

Coty hurried to pick up Erin, whose embarrassment added to the flushed cheeks caused by at least one too many drinks. She put one arm around him, but Ava took the load a second later and said,

"I'm lucky you don't weigh too much."

The grandfatherly gentleman who absorbed most of the spill pointed words in Ava's direction.

"Tell your twin to be like you and use better judgment."

"I will, sir. How much do we owe for the spilled drinks and cleaning bill?"

His grandmotherly partner said,

"Your mother would be proud of how you're helping her while offering to cover her mistake. That's payment enough. Merry Christmas, dear."

Everyone practiced silent diplomacy on the drive back to Ava's. Erin found something to say just before Coty cruised to a stop.

"I apologize for showing that when I can't hold my liquor, I can't hold myself up either. I promise you'll never see me like that again."

Shanelle's smile tried to cushion Erin's uneasy look by saying,

"Maybe we might if you ever impersonate a falling-down drunk at one of the city's comedy clubs."

"No thanks. I'll stick to the dancing scene."

Erin's metabolism burned through the residue fast enough for the sisters to mingle with Black Friday shoppers. Ava planned a convenient walking route that started 7 a.m. at Macy's in Herald Square, followed by Bloomingdales. From there, they hiked to some of the lower-end bargain stores. By the time they started walking back late that afternoon, Ava had taught Erin all about higher-versus-lower-end labels and department stores.

But Ava's talking and dusk descending obscured from her what Erin spied. A band of four muggers had just jumped out of a car not far ahead and began grabbing bags from shoppers.

Erin pulled Ava to a stop and hissed,

"Trouble's coming our way. Did you pack your pepper spray?"

"I did. Why?"

Erin pointed.

"Give it to me, and don't say we should run instead. Never turn your back on an attacker."

Erin charged into action as soon as she clutched the canister and shouted,

"Stay here. I'll find you."

Erin's bold move surprised the lead bad guy. The stinging spray hit him in both eyes, bringing him to his knees, and enough male shoppers joined the action to drive the others back into the car, which couldn't get away because of all the street traffic. By the time Erin hustled Ava away, the police had the event under control.

When they disappeared into a sandwich shop, Ava had recovered enough to say,

"We should have stayed. The police should know how you kept them from doing more damage."

Erin put a finger to her lips before saying,

"You never want to stand out in situations like this. It's safer to stay below the radar. Are you hungry enough for a sandwich?"

"How about a Coke and something sweet? That's an even better reward for avoiding danger."

Only Ava knew that her sister had cycled down for the Holidays, which meant no one at Dual Studios would detect Erin's completing her number one personal project: a Christmas-week agenda. While surfing the Web, she screen-scraped and copied information into a cheat sheet she printed when no one was watching.

Erin planned to make it the main topic at dinner on the Friday before Christmas. She handed a copy and gave Ava enough time to scan it before running through the bullet points.

Christmas-Week Cheat Sheet

You and I will:

- Watch the Rockettes Christmas Spectacular at Radio City Music Hall.
- Go to Christmas Eve Church Services at Saint Patrick's Cathedral.
- Go to Times Square for the New Year's Eve Ball Drop.
- Ride the Subway if the weather is bad. (I'll pack my map. You pack your pepper spray!)

Some fun facts:

- Radio City Music Hall is the largest indoor theatre in the world. Its marquee is a full city-block long. Its auditorium measures 160 feet from back to stage and the ceiling reaches a height of 84 feet. The walls and ceiling are formed by a series of sweeping arches that define a splendid and immense curving space.
- The Rockettes are an American precision dance company. Founded 1925 in St. Louis, they have performed since 1932 at the Radio City Music Hall in New York City

- There have been over 6,000 women who have performed as Rockettes since the New York Christmas Spectacular opening night in 1932] The Rockettes also conduct the Rockette Summer Intensive for dancers aspiring to be Rockettes.

- Saint Patricks, a Neo-Gothic Roman Catholic church, sits right in the heart of Fifth Avenue, which may look out of place from the surrounding shops, but that's what makes it beautiful! Dating all the way back to 1879, St. Patrick's Cathedral has become one of the city's most iconic landmarks, thanks to the exterior soaring spires, pointed arches, and intricate detailing that reflects the style of medieval European cathedrals. The interior is just as stunning too, with tons of stain glassed windows and an ornate altar. Midnight Mass at St. Patrick's Cathedral is a Christmas tradition dating back to 1879. It is arguably one of the most famous services in the world. The event is free, but it is ticketed to ensure the safety of the 2,500 people who pack the pews inside. And each year at an earlier service, our children tell the story of Christ's birth in drama and song. The service concludes with Communion, which all are welcome to receive. As a family-focused service, the music and length are family friendly.

"Watching the Rockettes at Radio City lets us check off two of NYC's iconic attractions. I've watched some videos for both, so now I can compare them to the real thing. Do you know if the old Electra ever saw it live?"

Ava shook her head sideways before saying,

"But even if my memory says we did, I'd want to go again."

"I say the same, and ditto for Christmas and New Year's Eve. I've already bought tickets or reserved our place at Saint Pats."

Erin's last words sparked Ava to say,

"As we saw on Black Friday, Christmas shopping is a major event, but I don't have anyone to shop for except you. What Christmas present would you like?"

"Now that's an easy question to answer. I don't know. How about you?"

"I like jewelry and perfume."

"Well, why don't you pick the stores and we can fit in shopping there this coming week? Pick out a couple of items, and I'll buy one of each, but I won't tell which. You'll see when you open your presents on Christmas Day."

"Why not on Christmas Eve? That'll make it even better."

The light workload let each sister daydream the afternoon before the Rockettes show. Erin thought the falling snow would add to the excitement, and it would give her additional practice for riding the subway. The entire evening exceeded her expectations, which she told herself on the ride home.

I'll lock tonight into my memory forever. From the giant marquee to the high-stepping Rockettes kicking like one on that magnificent stage, this is a night to remember.

Two nights later, lightly falling snow encouraged them to take the subway early enough so they could gaze at Saint Peter's glorious lighted facade. They stood among others, absorbing the magical view of its spires transcending the snowflakes and pointing toward the heavens.

Erin's enthusiasm bubbled out after the first service.

"I just loved seeing the joy of the kids telling this timeless Christmas Story and reminding their parents to always keep room in their hearts for others. We have to stay for the Midnight service. That'll guarantee a Christmas Eve to remember."

Ava looked as happy as her sister.

"We certainly should. We can compare them while going home. Besides, we shouldn't let free tickets go to waste."

When filing out after the Midnight Mass, Erin said,

"I'm stiff from sitting too long. Let's walk for a while and take in everything we see. We can make the comparisons at home."

The light snow still falling had put enough on the streets and sidewalks to make for slippery stepping, but Erin and Ava were wearing sure-footed running shoes. At this post-midnight hour, both auto and foot traffic were light, making their walk an almost private affair.

But that changed abruptly when a car coming their way skidded to a stop a quarter of a block ahead, and a woman leaped out from the rear door on the driver's side and started running toward them, followed in a flash by the driver.

The sisters were close enough to hear the big man yell,

"You ain't my bottom bitch, but I got you in my pocket, and you're my best for indoor pimping, so shut your mouth and get back in the car."

Ava stood frozen as they saw the man catch the woman and spin her around. She pushed to get out of his grip, but she couldn't run fast enough on her spikey shoes. He spun her around again and this time smashed his oversized fist into her nose, putting her splay-legged on her back.

Erin felt an overwhelming rage surge through every neural fiber in her brain, a rage she had never felt before, but it commanded her to act.

She yelled,

"Get your pepper spray ready," before sprinting toward the big brute.

Her speed caught him off guard. She kicked him in the groin, which doubled him up. Then she kicked again, but he didn't go down, so she started throwing punches, but his bulk kept them from doing much damage.

Then he started using his massive arms to block the blows and his sledgehammer fists to punch back, putting her on top of the woman who was struggling to get up. He bent down and kept punching until neither victim could move. Then he unzipped his fly.

His gloating voice boomed onto the empty sidewalk.

"Ha-ha-ha, I got two balls and a loaded bladder for you sluts."

But Ava charged into action, blindsiding him. Her pepper spray kept anything else from coming out. She kept spraying until the bully staggered backward before falling to the sidewalk. Erin struggled to her feet fast enough to finish him off, kicking enough times to smash his privates and front teeth.

The woman came to them while the sisters gasped for air. Ava yelled,

"Take off your stilettos if you want to run with us to the subway."

Erin led the way as fast as the footing would allow a bolt of lightning to fly.

Chapter 8
December 2193

"The Christmas Present"

Erin slowed enough to begin catching her breath while bounding two steps at a time down the stairs leading to the turn-style entrance. She dug out her card and went through as soon as Ava and the woman caught up, then hurried down another stairway leading to the train platform.

Once there, she looked all ways and heard nothing other than those in her head.

The platform's deserted...no trains approaching...and warm enough...it's time for Ava to check me out while I check the woman.

Ava's gentle fingers probed enough to find a still-bleeding split lip. She used four Kleenexes to stanch the flow; Erin kept pressing it so Ava could do the same to the woman's nose. Erin studied the patient while Ava did that.

I'd guess she's about my age, but she's no ordinary woman...she's a prostitute, but I'll use a more genteel term...demimonde...and gorgeous... long legs and an almost anorexic frame maybe an inch or two taller than my five-foot-ten measurement. Blonde hair and striking cheekbones tell me she might be Russian...Ava's about to speak...let's hear her diagnosis.

But before she could, the patient spoke first.

"You save me...Spaseeba... Thank you...I go."

The insouciant and husky accent that just rolled out told Erin she could only have come from Russia.

Ava's worried-sounding words came next.

"You've got a broken nose that needs to be set right now. We have to get you to an E.R."

"Nyet. Nyet I.D."

Ava didn't make any reply, so Erin did. Speaking slowly, she said,

"My name is Erin Keenan, and my sister's name is Ava. What is your name."

"I Oksana Androva from Roosha."

"I thought so. We are twenty-five. I think you might be our age."

Oksana nodded before saying,

"You smart."

"OK, we'll take you to our condo and then figure out what to do next."

The next words came from Erin forty-five minutes later, after Ava packed a washcloth with ice and kept pressing it to Oksana, who was now sitting at the kitchen table.

"We have to set your nose before it swells too much. If it does, I won't be able to snap it back into place."

Ava removed the washcloth, revealing a blue-eyed and fearful-looking beauty.

"You doktor?"

"No, but I'll figure it out. Wait here."

Erin hurried back less than a minute later, positioning her laptop where she could see it and Oksana. Ava moved a couple of steps behind her sister.

The tension built with every minute until Erin broke the silence.

"I can set your nose to look as good as new. Ava, would you happen to have a bottle containing lidocaine or cocaine in an epinephrine solution? Some long nasal swabs would be helpful too."

"No."

"I didn't think so, but that's OK. Please bring some duct tape, scissors, two towels, a hand mirror, and a pan of water. When you come back, I'll wash my hands."

All hands were back five minutes later. Erin stood directly in front of Oksana and spoke as calmly as she could.

"Please lock your eyes onto mine while I explain what I'm going to do. Your nose is bent to your left, which is my right. I will press each hand palms down on your cheeks and position my thumbs tight against your nose. Ava, I need you to stand behind Oksana and hold her head steady."

Erin said more after Ava took her position.

"I am going to snap your nose to the right to put it back in place. I might need to do a couple of snaps to get the alignment just right. You might hear some snapping, crackling, and popping but don't think about it. It's normal. Now close your eyes, and on the count of three, I'll do the first snap."

As soon as Oksana closed her eyes, Erin lip-spoke to Ava.

"I'll do it on the count of two," before speaking loudly but calmly.

"Everyone looks ready. Here we go. ONE... TWO."

Even Ava heard the snap while feeling Oksana shudder. Erin studied her handiwork as fast as she could before issuing her next command.

"Now I will snap to your left. Ava, hold Oksana's head as tight as you can."

When she snapped her eyes shut, expecting to hear another count, Erin lip-spoke,

"I'm snapping NOW."

This time, Ava heard a crraackkle that gave Oksana another shudder. Erin saw she needed another snap to the left and signaled to Ava they would repeat the procedure.

A distinct pop told Erin she had made the alignment. She stepped back and said,

"Ava, use the mirror to show Oksana how her nose looks after you wipe away the blood."

Oksana looked long enough for a tiny smile to replace her pent-up stress.

"Spaseeba... Thank you."

"Good. Now, here's the final step. You will lie down on my bed and try to sleep while I press an ice-filled washcloth against your nose. And then, when you wake up, we'll put tape across it. So, let's do it right now."

When enough light had filtered into Erin's personal space, her brain snapped awake, explaining the situation. She had fallen asleep. Her head rested on a now empty bed while her body slumped forward from a chair.

She groped for the bedside lamp, and when she clicked it on, saw the source of an indistinct noise, galvanizing her to shout,

"Oksana, what are you looking for?"

The light and sound stopped her hands from digging deeper into the drawers of the desk she was kneeling at.

"Need manee dollar…Need coke."

Erin was about to shout again, but Ava slipped into the room and lifted Oksana before talking loud and slow while using hand gestures.

"The guy who punch you, is he your john? Did he hook you on coke?"

"Da."

Ava's look told Erin to say something.

"Can you take me to the place you buy coke?"

"Da."

"OK. Ava, put a warmer coat and running shoes on her. I'll suit up and pack a purse. Meet me at the front door."

Erin spoke again ten minutes later, using few loud words and gestures.

"We take subway to place. Then point to john. I do talking. Do you understand?"

"Da."

Erin grabbed her hand; out they went.

Jolts occurring as Erin's brain elevated her to a state of awareness that once again united her mind and body. She didn't need to say anything until Oksana stopped next to a car parked at the corner of dingy deserted streets. When the driver flipped on parking lights and rolled down his window, Erin knew what to say and do when the driver said,

"Who are you?"

"This is my friend, Oksana. She says you can fix us up."

"Oksana, huh. I know a guy named John she works for. Whatcha need?"

"Some coke and needles."

"How much?"

"Enough for a couple of days."

When the driver flipped on the interior lights, Erin saw everything she needed: only two men in the car; the guy in the passenger's seat holding a bag. They talked for a minute before the driver poked his head out the window and said,

"What a nice Christmas present. We can handle that. Maybe we'll give you a discount if she hops into the back seat after you pay. Show me the money and we'll negotiate."

"Let me get it out of my purse."

Erin didn't need to speak again. Her hand reached in slowly and then paused as if she were fishing for a wad of bills. And then she began moving at the speed of lightning. She whipped her hand out and shoved it and whatever it was holding at the driver.

Bang-bang. Bang-bang. Erin fired two bullets each at her targets. The geysers of blood told her they wouldn't move. She shoved her gun into her purse and leaned far enough in to grab the bag and pull it out.

It took only one quick look. The bag contained plenty of rock crack and everything needed to shoot up. Erin also found a bonus: wads of money. She zipped it shut and knew what to do next.

Clutching purse and bag in a life-or-death grip, she pivoted before shouting,

"We got what you need. Now we run home."

Oksana clutched Erin's hand all the way there.

Chapter 9
December 2193

"Room in the Heart"

Erin awoke in a flash when Ava shook her, still feeling energized from last night's harrowing adventure. She sat up and spoke first, noticing Oksana standing alongside.

"Good morning. I hope both of you are feeling better. It looks like you've cleaned up our guest and put duct tape on her nose. And from the looks of it, I guess you helped her shoot up. What else do you want to tell me?"

Ava talked while Oksana focused on every word.

"She's fixed for now. And she figured out how to get the language translator on my cellphone working. She's smart and understands English much better than she speaks. Why don't you freshen up, and then the three of us can talk? I have a lot of questions, and you probably have more."

"You can start now, and I'll join in after running. If the weather's OK, I'll run through Central Park."

Erin suited up, and she knew as soon as she started jogging toward the park that the weather was better than OK. The cloudless blue sky on a brisk, windless day energized her even more. When she reached the southeast corner of the park, she headed north on a two-lane running and biking path that bordered it.

She built speed gradually, noticing a continual procession of joggers running in small groups. The dusting of snow didn't bother them, but she thought it explained why she saw few bikers. But the snow didn't bother the dog walkers. Their pets raced through the snow faster than any runner.

Erin ran by herself. She wanted no interruptions while talking to herself. The further she ran, the faster her thinking became. Alisha came out to remind her about the other kind of speed.

"You're running fast enough. If you speed up, the other runners will think you're showing off. You can even slow the pace so you can enjoy right now even more."

Erin took her alter-ego's advice, and by the time she reached home, she knew she had figured out a win-win-win path for the New Year, and she also knew what next to do.

She put on some leisure clothes after showering and went to the kitchen, where she found Ava doing most of the talking to a somber-looking Oksana.

She quartered an orange before sitting down and looking at Ava.

Ava switched from questioning Oksana to giving answers she knew Erin wanted.

"So, here's Oksana's story. She comes from Moscow, where she lived with her parents. The father needed her to help take of the mother and give him as much money as she could, but she couldn't find jobs that paid enough because she never graduated from high school. She's smart, but not book smart, and when a sex trafficker noticed her body four years ago, he paid her way to New York and promised that her pimp would take care of her and send money back home. How do you like her pimp's name, Humphrey Dickstein?"

"I can think of a fitting nickname. How do you like 'Humper?' It sort of connects his first name to his career."

"His ladies might, but they came up with one that's twice as good, 'Humpy the Dickhead.' Both hit the nail on the head."

"We could turn that cliché into something more fitting, but tell me what he did for her."

"Well, he didn't get her fake I.D.s, but he did get her hooked on coke to control her. That's what he does to all his ladies. They live in small groups at rundown apartment buildings where he charges rents that eat up most of their dough. That's what I know so far. What should I ask her next?"

"Don't ask, tell her this. She must keep her mouth shut about last night, and she can never go back to wherever she's staying, not even to pick up her stuff. Does she know that?"

"That's where we left off. What should we do next?"

"You both look ready for something else. Why don't you take her to McDonald's and then go to a movie, but don't stay away too long. And pick one that'll help her English. While you're doing that, I'll come up with a plan that we'll talk about when you get back."

Twenty minutes later, Erin had the kitchen all to herself. She fired up her laptop and contacted her number-one consultant. Indira's GUI appeared, waiting for Erin to speak.

"Hello, Indira. I'm calling because I now have things to talk about other than questions. I'll start with the easiest item first for which I don't need your help. I'm working as an intern for Ava at her company. I like her associates, the industry, and the company, which I suppose you already know."

"That's the fashion industry's Dual Flying Design Studios. But I must ask, what happened to your interest in Strike Force Security Services?"

"They took a pass on hiring me until I get more experience, which I'm getting at Dual Studios. And this leads to the second item. I don't need your help this minute, but I might in the future. People like my researching and blogging skills. I'm already using them at Dual, and I see how I can leverage them for my very own business. But that's for later."

"Well then, for what do you need my help?"

"I've created a situation that's currently under control. Ava and I just came across a Russian demimonde that a sex trafficker snuck into America four years or so ago. She's my age and needs our help. And for starters, all I need from you is what you already did for Ava and me—a set of fake I.D.s, like a green card or some sort of company sponsorship. Her real name is Oksana Androva, but we'll change it to Ivana Romanova so the pimps and drug dealers from her past can't find her. What can you do for us?"

"Not only will I create a green card and company sponsorship documentation, but I will place them in all government files to satisfy its intrusive snooping."

"What company will you use?"

"One of my own, of course. I would ask you to pick one, but you don't remember any of them. Describe her to me and I will choose the optimal one."

"Six-feet tall, long legs on an almost anorexic physique, and classic European facial features including high cheekbones, pale skin, blonde hair, thin nose, and blue oval eyes. And she's got this insouciant, husky Russian accent that just rolls out. It's as sexy as the way she looks when she tarts up."

"I will decide now. She will be working for my Los Angeles-based company—Trans-Entertainment. And instead of your asking for additional I.D.s, I will prepare a complete set that will make her a naturalized citizen who qualifies for social security and all government health benefits. I will also give her a high school diploma plus a state-of-New-York driver's license. Regarding finances, she will have an Amazon Prime credit card issued by Chase, where she has savings and credit accounts. But I will make all the Chase accounts joint. They will have adequate funds in the bank accounts, but you and Oksana will be the joint owners."

"No-no. Make them joint between Ava and Oksana. Other than that, you've thought of everything. When will you have the accounts set up and the actual I.D.s ready?"

"As soon as Ava Emails me Oksana's vital statistics along with a photo attached. Indy-M will collect all of them and then Fed-Ex the set to Ava's home address. That will be safer than drone delivery. And I must ask a final question; where will Oksana live?"

"With Ava and me for the time being."

Erin detected the tone of Indira's words had suddenly softened, becoming playful instead of didact, when she replied.

"Excellent. I am pleased that I had to ask you questions rather than the opposite. I will contact you if I need exegesis. And for the time being, you have enough to lead a conversation with your roommates, which indicates our singular Chautauquas are starting to empower you. Please carry on."

Indira's GUI vanished before Erin could get in a final word, so she spoke to herself instead.

I hope the old Electra appreciated Indira as much as I do. And she must have been smarter than me. Maybe playing Indira's word games will make me smarter. Well, I better check what exegesis and Chautauqua mean. And I can surf the Web for them. Who needs a memory anyway?

Erin worked nonstop to finish a write-up she needed for a meeting with her roommates. Finishing just in time, she buttonholed them as soon as they came home.

"Come to the kitchen as soon as you can. I want to explain the plan I've mapped out."

Erin popped a can of Coke before sitting at the table, and she started talking to Ava as soon as they sat.

"When speaking to Oksana, remember to speak loud and slow, OK?"

Ava's nod said she would. Erin proceeded.

Here's your copy of our plan. I want you to read it to her a couple of times after I'm done, but right now, I need to explain it to you. Take a minute to read it, and when you're ready, I'll walk you through it."

Erin slid it to Ava.

Our Care-filled Plan for Turning
Oksana Andropova into Ivana Romanova

We three swear to keep everything that happened on Christmas and everything in this plan a secret. She can never return to her old apartment or contact old friends. If someone says they recognize her, tell them they're wrong.

Oksana will stay with us until she is ready to be on her own. She has a new name because she is leaving her old life behind. Ivana Romanova is a naturalized U.S. citizen and will soon have a set of all I.D.s, certificates, and accounts that the average American needs.

Here are Erin's Responsibilities:

1. Medicate her off coke.
2. Improve her English.
3. Improve her nutrition and exercise programs.
4. Improve her view of life.
5. Tell Ava what careers Oksana might like.

Here are Ava's Responsibilities:

1. Do a cosmetics and hairstyle makeover.
2. Get her new clothes and shoes.
3. Send to our consultant Oksana's vital statistics and a photo. Our consultant will create all the necessary documents.
4. Ava will receive ASAP a Fed Ex packet from our consultant containing all necessary I.D.s, certificates, documents, etc. When she gets it, she will explain how Oksana should use them.
5. Help Oksana find a new career and prepare a resume she can use to get job interviews.
6. Ava will help Oksana send money each month to her parents.

She signaled by nodding that Erin could continue, so she did by saying,

"Before I start, I want to tell you the sleeping arrangements. Oksana sleeps in your bedroom. The two of you can decide on the details. Are you OK with that?"

"Of course. It has more room than your sleeper sofa."

"Fine and dandy. Now, please give your general thoughts before asking questions."

"Thanks for giving me a chance to say something. I like the title. It shows what a smart wordsmith you are, which Pat really likes. And it also shows how thoroughly you organize things. That's why you're such a good Internet snooper. And I can't think of anything else we need to keep secret. Can I now ask you some questions?"

"Please do."

"I can make a guess that our consultant is Indira. Am I right?'

"You bet. Keep going."

"How'd you come up with the new name? Why not let Oksana do that?"

"It's a sexy name that matches her looks, and I didn't want to waste time talking about something I can pick faster and better by myself."

"OK, I agree. What about all the I.D.s and documents and things?"

"I'll answer what I think is the most important piece, which is all about the money. She will have a credit card along with savings and checking accounts. They are joint accounts with you, so you can control how much she spends. When you get the Fed Ex packet, you'll see how much money's in them. You can figure out all the other items when you go through the packet.

"And here's the last thing. She's officially working for one of Indira's companies, Trans-Entertainment, based in Los Angeles. Her checking account will get credited each month with her salary.

"I hope that's your last question. I've run out of mental energy. I'm going for another run while you and Oksana go over the plan. Maybe we can talk some more if I feel like it when I get back."

Ava smiled for the first time since she sat down.

"Go right now and please come back at least partially energized."

Erin ran hard right from the start, following the same route she had run that morning, hoping this combination would unwind some of the mental-draining tension. And it worked. By the time she returned, she felt like she could run forever.

Oksana left Ava in the kitchen when she heard Erin come in. She stopped when they came face-to-face. Erin waited for her to speak.

A timid smile accompanied her hushed words.

"You and your sister make place in heart for me. I make place in mine for you two too."

Then her soft lips lingered on Erin's cheek, which she returned with a comforting hug. Hoping the hug and the kiss would empower her wish that the love she was feeling and sending soul reeling would dwell in her heart forever.

As she fell asleep that night, Alisha whispered they would.

73

Chapter 10
February 2194

"A Trio of New Moves"

During the first two months of the year, Erin had begun implementing her plan for the year by using three activities: working with Ava to build Ivana's new life, using her Dual Studios assignments to outline an entrepreneurial Life Coach business she could run, and testing some of its services on Ava.

Erin coached herself before making a long overdue online call to Indira.

I've read and watched enough to know the basics. Life Coaching is an unregulated, loosely structured industry. Anyone can set up their own online business with or without taking a certification course. I'll win clients by making their first session free, and in it, I'll build rapport, set goals, and set follow-up action steps.

And I know how to build it. I'll set it up so it runs completely online, then get it registered, design my client recruiting to focus on females, do all advertising via Social Media, and consult only via the Internet.

And I'm finally ready to get Indira's assessment, but I'll make another request first. I hope she doesn't find them too difficult. Well, no sense delaying further. I'll power up my laptop and do it now.

Erin thought she would start the conversation, but Indira surprised her by speaking first.

"Hello, Erin. You haven't contacted me since Christmas Day, which indicates you have made substantial progress. Now, you are contacting me on February 29th, a day that occurs only in a Leap Year. That tells me you must have an unusual request. Please tell me what it is."

Erin pretended she remembered all about Leap Year by simply avoiding any mention when she replied.

"I have two, actually, and I'll describe the most limiting one first. Three roommates in a Manhattan-size one-bedroom condo gives us hardly enough room to change our minds, and even then, we must take turns. When I checked condo availability early this month, I learned there are several for subleasing or purchase. You already own the one we're living in. Do you own any of the others?"

"I do. What are your intentions?"

"I would like Ava and Ivana to move into a two-bedroom unit while I stay put. Do you have one available?"

"I do, but it's unfurnished."

"Not a problem. Ava has interior design instincts. She and Ivana can furnish it gradually, using their salaries to do that. Will you transfer ownership to Ava?"

"Do not concern yourself. I will arrange all financial matters with the property manager. Your roommates will become erstwhile whenever they choose to move next week. I will Email her the documents she can sign online."

"How will she know the unit number?"

"You tell me."

"Uh, umm…OK, I got it. It will be in the documents."

Indira paused for Erin to make a clever reply, but her crestfallen look said she couldn't. Instead, she said,

"I must disappoint you. I'm a dullard when it comes to playing your word games. None of the old Electra's vocabulary transcended into my brain. And I don't know what erstwhile roommates are."

Indira's empathy sounded in her voice.

"Ava and Ivana become your former roommates, analogous to your becoming the former Electra. And contrary to being disappointed, you have exceeded my expectations. Your empathy for Ivana and your searching the Internet in lieu of memory is admirable. So, be happy, and now tell me your second request."

Erin's enthusiasm flashed back to life.

"I want to start a Life Coaching business. It's the practically perfect business for me, because even though I know absolutely nothing about the detailed services, my searching skills will make me a quick study, and I've already researched how to set it up. A name and GUI are the only missing pieces, and I can figure that out. Please tell me what you think?"

"I will as soon as you tell me what your Unique Selling Proposition is."

"One of the links led me to a useful diagram illustrating what USP is. It had three overlapping circles, the first labeled what I do well, the second for what my competition does well, and the third for what my target market wants. My USP sits in the best place on the diagram, and I'm better there than the competition because Ava and Ivana can tell me what females want, and I use use brain science and ChatGPT to make my services better than anyone else's. Now will you tell me?"

"I shall do better than that. I shall show you your GUI, complete with a suitable name. Reply when ready."

Indira scrolled it on the screen as soon she stopped talking.

The Transcendental Life Coach
For Dual Females Everywhere

"AI-Empowerment for the Dual You"

We provide Transcendent ChatGPT GUI Interfaces for:

- Trans-Investing: AI-Empowered Portfolio Management that matches Your Goals

- Trans-Life Coaching: Goal-Centered Meditative Counseling

- Trans-Gaming: Beyond State-of-The-Art Gambling Platform

- Trans-Artistry: Virtual Reality Enhancements to Your Audio-Visual Image

- Trans Age-Beauty Life-styling: Nutrition and Exercise for Age-Deceleration
- Trans-Entertainment: Novels and Screenwriting Development Modeling

Click on Each Bullet for more details.

Click here for the Introductory Video: ___

YOU Hold the Transcendental Power in your Personal World. Please contact us when You are ready to transcend your limits!

Erin blinked several times after sitting back, studied the GUI for several minutes, and then leaned in to reply.

"Let me try to show you I'm not a complete dullard. I surmise that the old Electra might have added 'Life Coach' to her resume. If so, you adjusted her GUI to fit my situation via your clever wordplay. I love the name and the portfolio of consulting services I'll offer. I don't yet know any particular areas of consulting I want to focus on, but I do know this—the old Electra's never coming back. I don't think I can ever come close to what she was, but that won't worry me; what I can't remember can't hurt me. I'll figure out the consulting details when I figure out what interests jibe with whatever talents I now have."

"Of course you will. And in the process, you will find that what you have become is extraordinary in its singular way. I will also teach you that everyone can say the same if they stop to think about it."

"Thanks for saying that, and I say thank you, thank you, and I'll take it from here."

"Excellent. Carry on, dear, and never fear. You shall always be my favorite mere mortal. I trust I have made that clear."

Indira's GUI disappeared, leaving Erin speechless until she spoke to herself.

I don't think even the old Electra could match that. Neither can ChatGPT, so I won't bother trying. I have better things to do. I think I'll listen to some of the classic retro rock sung by those females whose voices are as enticing as the way they move. After doing that, I'll carry on. And after I share some of Indira's good news, I think Ava will too.

Ava had kept as busy as Erin ever since Ivana had fallen into their lives, literally as well as actually, but her point of view showed different aspects of shared interests.

She enjoyed working at the office while Erin worked from home, medicating Ivana off cocaine. Ivana's pain stabbed her heart even during dinner conversations when Erin praised Ivana for stoically refusing a coke injection that would ease her withdrawal symptoms.

But she loved watching how Erin's diet and exercise regimen put more weight and definition in all the right places, which added to the striking beauty coming from the hair styling and cosmetics makeover Ava gave her, and when Ivana started wearing the clothes she brought home, Ivana looked more striking than any of the females parading around at Dual Studios.

And most of all, she loved just talking to her, helping improve her English while learning about her life in Moscow but keeping her most intimate wishes to herself.

I feel a bond growing with Ivana… The three of us are becoming a family. I love Erin, and my feelings toward Ivana are similar but at the same time different. It's too soon to ask Ivana how she feels. She has to work through all the trauma her previous lifestyle forced on her. She'll show me someday when she's ready.

Ava knew a new month had just rolled in because when logging on first thing when getting to her Dual Studios cubical, her Email account showed today's date, March 1, 2024. It also contained an Email sent late last night from Indira, which gave a welcome surprise.

I have arranged for you and Oksana to move into an unfurnished two-bedroom condo in the building any day starting next week, which works well. You'll have the weekend to shop for furniture. Erin didn't mention anything about it before you left for work this morning, so make it the number one topic at dinner tonight.

Erin and Ivana had dinner waiting when she arrived. After putting her coat in the entry closet, she splashed water on her face and hands before hurrying to the kitchen.

Judging from the way Erin started tonight's table talk, it seemed she thought today was a typical Thursday, so Ava let her and Ivana do most of the talking until she found a place to change the subject.

"Isn't it wonderful how quickly Ivana's English has improved in only two months? It shows what a great language coach Erin is."

By now, Ivana knew whenever her roommates left a long pause, she should talk.

"Da, yes, but you big help too when we talk about I.D.s and me and job I can do."

"I'll take some of the credit, but I'd like to find out how much credit she gets for an Email I read this morning. Erin, what do you know about the condo Ivana and I will move into next week?"

Ava could tell she knew a lot, though she tried to hide it behind a quizzical look.

"Not much. I don't even know the unit number. Why don't you provide exegesis. I know you know it's a big synonym for the noun that means 'explanation.' So please tell us."

Ava told just enough to keep it simple while at the same time pleasing Ivana, who spoke five minutes later."

"You pick stores. We shop Saturday."

Erin said,

"I'll come along to make sure you buy only what you need to settle in, so both of you should settle down until Saturday…"

Ava picked the Manhattan Ikea store that featured a design studio and associates who could recommend what to buy. She liked the minimalist Scandinavian style that made self-assembly easy.

By mid-afternoon, Ava and Ivana took the recommendation, buying only a round kitchen table and four Breuer chairs, two queen-sized beds, and a pillow-backed three-cushion, dark gray sofa with additional pillows on its armrests. The store promised mid-morning Wednesday delivery.

The trio paced themselves on Monday and Tuesday evenings when hauling clothes, kitchenware, and miscellany to their unit, which was three floors below. Ava took Wednesday off, and with help from Erin and the delivery driver, they had a livable setup by mid-afternoon. After stocking the kitchen with enough breakfast items to last until the weekend, the trio celebrated by going to a local pizza place.

Saying goodnight by nine that evening, Erin let them enjoy a special moment. The thrill of having a two-bedroom condo all to themselves chased away any fatigue, so they sat leaning against one another on the sofa, placed against a wall perpendicular to the windows. City light and softly glowing lamps added to the ambiance.

Ava felt an emotional tingle caused by Ivana's body heat, and it made her wish the dawn would never come. She sat perfectly still until Ivana cautiously put one hand in Ava's lap. Ava responded by turning enough to make holding it in both of hers comfortable, and then, with words as quiet as the night, said,

"Now we have a place our friends can visit."

She felt Ivana lean lightly against her and, sensing she would speak, turned more so she could synch Ivana's lips and words. They came slowly, hesitantly.

"You and sister pretty. Have guy-friends?"

"No, not in a dating way."

Ava knew Ivana was searching for the right words to touch an intimate subject, so she tried to help.

"I'm not against sex, but guys can be so blunt. Ladies are smoother and much more subtle. That's why I like them better."

Ava could feel Ivana's tiny tremble just before she took one of Ava's hands in both of hers and placed a delicate kiss on each finger. Then she used both of hers to bring Ava's into her lap before whispering,

"I like ladies too. Pretty ladies like you."

Then she moved into a comfortable position that touched torso and thigh.

Ava's quiet tears accompanied her silent prayer.

May we lie through the night till dawn brightens the sky.

Chapter 11
April 2194

"Help Wanted"

Alonzo's pulse jumped as fast as the pit in his stomach plunged into his genitals, causing a double emotional jolt that he knew would intensify when opening an Email from a source he dared not oppose. And he would have to read at lightning speed because these Emails always self-destructed, leaving nary a trace.

Alonzo steeled his nerves as he prepared to read it early in his office on the first day of April before Eve and Nila strolled in.

To: Alonzo Cortez
From: Indira
Subject: Termination of Strike Force Services
Date: April 1ˢᵗ, 2024

Effective immediately, I am terminating your Strike Force Services consulting business that you have run for twenty-two years. I have appreciated your dedication to Electra Kirchner and adherence to our confidentiality agreement that binds you to complete secrecy regarding the nature of your previous assignments, as well as our relationship.

Certain information has recently come to my knowledge that Electra Kirchner will not return, which means the scope of Strike Force Services is irrelevant. Therefore, I have decommissioned your robo-soldiers and agents by deactivating their control software. Please return them to the Deus Lab no later than April 15th.

I will extend your Custodian Contract for Ms. Kirchner's property to January 1st, 2025, at which time I will let you know if your services will still be required.

My decision is final. Do not reach out to me. I will contact you if you have relevant experience that might fit future needs.

Best wishes.

Alonzo's brain seized up. He knew that no amount of mood elevators could lift him from the stunned state he was sitting in.

Eve pointed to him when she and Nila came in at 8:15.

"It looks like he just got some stunning news. We better find out what's going on."

When his sisters sat facing him, Alonzo stirred enough to show he had not taken any stupor-inducing drugs. Nila looked at Eve, which was her cue to speak.

"Don't do a diplomatic dance around what's troubling you. Just tell us what the problem is."

"We're out of business. I have to return all our androids."

Eve's eyes opened so wide that Nila thought she would need to jam her palms over them to keep from shooting out. When the risk subsided, she said,

"Could this be some kind of April Fool's joke?"

"No, and don't ask me why."

Eve's voice sounded an alarm.

"What'll we use for protection guards? What are we going to do?"

"Adapt or die. Start coming up with some ideas, and start by trying to salvage some of our current business. We'll talk when you have something."

Erin usually had creative ideas churning. Those most immediate would need Ava and Ivana to implement, and the trio would discuss them at her home office on this early mid-April evening as soon as Ava returned from work.

Erin let Ava begin with chitchat after exchanging Russian-style greetings with Ivana before sitting down.

Her fresh-sounding voice pleased Erin almost as much as it did for the Russian beauty.

"You've turned the place into a combination office and living quarters. You've been telling us about starting a consulting business, and you can run it from here while still working for Dual Studios. Are you ready to launch it?"

"I already have. This'll be the first time for you and Ivana to see its Website, so take a look."

Erin scrolled its GUI onto the screen, then waited long enough for Ava to explain it to Ivana before proceeding.

The Transcendental Life Coach
For Dual Females Everywhere

"AI-Empowerment for the Dual You"

We provide Transcendent ChatGPT GUI Interfaces for:
- Trans-Investing: AI-Empowered Portfolio Management that matches Your Goals

- Trans-Life Coaching: Goal-Centered Meditative Counseling

- Trans-Gaming: Beyond State-of-The-Art Gambling Platform

- Trans-Artistry: Virtual Reality Enhancements to Your Audio-Visual Image

- Trans Age-Beauty Life-styling: Nutrition and Exercise for Age-Deceleration

- Trans-Entertainment: Novels and Screenwriting Development   Modeling

Click on Each Bullet for more details.

Click here for the Introductory Video: ___

YOU Hold the Transcendental Power in your Personal World. Please contact us when You are ready to transcend your limits!

Erin waited for Ava to ask her first question.

"How did you learn so much about all these topics?"

"I haven't done that yet, but as soon as I sign up a client, I simply need to stay a step or two ahead of her."

"Do you have any clients yet?"

"I hope to recruit my first two this evening, Ivana and you. Are you ready to hear more?"

Using her combination of improvised Russian phrases and body language, Ava made sure Ivana understood. Both of them looked eager for Erin to say more.

"Ivana and I are already doing the life-styling stuff, and just look at the results. She's firmed up and gone from looking emaciated to the gaunt look that high-fashion runway models have. And this'll take us to the entertainment piece where you fit in. You can get her a modeling interview at Dual."

"How can I do that? I know nothing about modeling."

"I'll be your consultant for that, and here's your first lesson. I didn't put it in a scrollable chart, but take a look at what I jotted down."

Erin handed it to Ava, who shared it with Ivana.

A Primer on Modeling

Modeling Market Segments:
- High-Fashion Runway

- Commercial

- Fitness

- Beauty (Headshots)

- Swimwear and Lingerie

How to Learn the Skills:
- In-person and Online Modeling Classes

- On-the-Job Training

How to get Hired:
Put together a Presentation Package:
- Resume

- Runway Video

- Personality Video Interview

- Vital Stats Sheet—Ethnicity Age Height   Weight Dimensions Shoe-size   Photo Gallery

When Hired by a Modeling Agency:
- You Model Their Clothing

- They send you to Casting Calls

Challenges:
- Maintaining Body Weight and Proportions

- Dodging Sexual Predators

Erin interrupted them sooner than they might have liked.

"The two of you can study it later, but here's the starting point. Ava can assemble the presentation package that'll contain Ivana's resume showing her modeling credentials and employment history. Then, when you're ready, Ava can have Pat introduce her to Dual's modeling department. It's obvious she's got the look of a runway model."

Ava spoke for a puzzled-looking Ivana as well as herself.

"But what about teaching her?"

Erin's wry smile lasted long enough to make the point before she said,

"She already walks the walk. Why do you think Humpy didn't want to let her walk away? And if she needs more coaching, you can show her some online videos. How does that sound?"

Ivana surprised Erin by speaking up.

"Da, I like. Ava and I watch video tonight."

Ava looked ready to go.

"But let's have dinner first. Ivana and I will throw something on the table. You join us in about a half hour."

"Excellent. That gives me plenty of time to send an Email."

Alonzo's mood hadn't rebounded during the two weeks after Indira's Email. Neither he nor his sisters had come up with anything that might keep them afloat, and it depressed him to the point of ignoring most Emails.

But he still summoned the energy to drag himself and his sisters every day to the office to maintain a disciplined professional schedule. He convinced himself to empty his Email inbox first thing on the last Friday of the month.

He charged into his sisters' cubical moments after reading another shocking Email.

"Guess who sent me an Email? No, don't guess, I'll tell you. That Erin Keenan."

Eve grimaced.

"You mean the candidate we flushed months ago? What does she want?"

"She just told me she's happy working at Dual Flying Design Studios, and she's also starting a consulting business."

"So what? What'll that do for us?"

Nila spoke, hoping to calm her sister down.

"I think Alonzo should call her. It's always good to find out what others are thinking."

"Both of you come to my office. I'll get her on speakerphone right now."

Erin knew what to say when an unexpected call came in from a name she recognized.

"Good morning, Alonzo. This is Erin Keenan at Transcendental Services. How may I assist you?"

"Erin, this is Alonzo Cortez. I and my sisters have you on speaker. I want to congratulate you."

"Thanks. Everything here is full speed ahead. How are you?"

"Uh, well, we've hit a rough patch and have to close down Strike Force, which means we're looking for ways to salvage our consulting business. I thought we might share ideas and maybe come up with something that's a win-win."

"That will depend on the experience you have. What areas do you have in mind?"

"We have loads of DC consulting experience that connects politics to climate change and NASA. Would that be of interest?"

"It might, so here's my preliminary offer. You and your sisters will work for me. Keep your DC office open, but change the name to Transcendental Services and adjust your Website so it connects with mine, which has transcentallifecoaching.com for its URL. Do you follow so far?"

Eve interrupted before Alonzo could answer.

"Hello, Ms. Keenan. This is Eve Cortez. So, we're now working for you as a subsidiary? What about money?"

"Becoming a subsidiary is a painless transition, and you have no out-of-pocket costs other than rent and Internet charges. I will pay them on a month-by-month basis. It will be specified in the contract we sign, as will our revenue split on the client projects you bring in. And I'll be very generous. You keep 85 percent, and I will cover any expenses necessary to launch them. I will also participate if my skills fit. Don't you think all this is fair?"

Alonzo wrestled the reply away.

"I do, but shouldn't we meet in person?"

"No, we already did that. The contract I'll send will include the points I've made. All you have to do is sign it and send me the info so I can set up paying your monthly charges."

"OK, but when will we meet again?"

"I'll come to DC as soon as you have a client project. And please call me at the start of each month so I know what's going on. I've got a call coming in, so bye-bye for now."

The abrupt disconnect stopped everyone, but Eve spoke seconds later.

"I think I might have been wrong about Keenan. She's got more experience than I thought."

Alonzo said,

"OK, we'll meet in the conference room after a mood elevator break and start listing our top clients for potential projects. Let's see where this leads."

Zoltan Sultani never needed mood elevators because he knew how to adapt rather than die. This flexibility let him play the "long political game"—a strength that China subtly wielded against America, the impulsive, headstrong leader of the West. The Bigger Brother Conspiracy did too, as did Xinquian Hung, the leader of its covert Gang of Three-Plus-One organization.

No matter which administration strutted in the halls of Congress, Zoltan always stepped carefully and convincingly enough to gain a seat among the powerful elite.

Twenty years ago, he had failed to hunt down an Electra Kirchner. She had always kept several steps ahead. Spying on Strike Force Security had been the closest he had ever come, but the Kirchner trail had vanished twenty years ago.

At first, Zoltan tightened his Strike Force snooping, but as the days morphed into months and then into years, he curtailed it to a once-a-month assignment he gave to one of Xing's automated ChatGPT snooping apps. And tonight, he would toast himself.

Ah-ha…Alonzo Cortez has shut down Strike Force Services. Might this mean the Kirchner target has come back? Time will tell, and I will gradually deploy intrusion assets. My long-game approach serves me well.

Zoltan lost count of the number of scotch and soda toasts he served himself that night. He knew he had refilled his glass at least twice, and each time using less of the soda and ice.

Chapter 12
June 2194

"The Starting Project Lineup"

Erin always enjoyed having dinner every Friday at Ava and Ivana's condo for a variety of reasons. She would use the first one in June to summarize all she had accomplished during the last four weeks.

Seeing her eagerness, Ava skipped the usual small talk and let Erin lead off.

"I officially landed my first life coaching client today. She's a Chinese news reporter working in Washington. She called me last week after visiting my Website. Well, I got an Email today scheduling her first online coaching session for next week on Tuesday. It shows that Social Media advertising works. I should get more calls this month, and I can pick and choose to fit in with my other projects. Maybe there's one that you two might want me to start if Dual doesn't hire Ivana. When do you introduce her to Pat?"

"Ivana says she's ready, so I'll ask Pat to pick a day next week. And let's let Ivana tell you how ready she is."

"Ava and I rehearse what I say when give him presentation packet. Then Ava take me to modeling department if he like."

Erin said,

"He will, but suppose you decide you don't want to do modeling work. Have you thought about something else?"

"Yes, but need you and Ava help. What you think about battered hooker survivor group?"

Both looked at Erin.

"I'll have to surf the Web to find out, but tell me, what do you have in mind?"

"We start by finding one come from Russia to City, get them away from pimp, and help recover. Then find more."

"This has possibilities. Let me do my research and then come up with a plan."

Erin didn't ask for Ava's opinion. Her look of caution said she was about to speak up.

"It's a touching gesture, but we better be careful when we go looking for them. I don't think any of the johns will recognize Ivana, but they'll be suspicious about what we're doing."

"You're right. I'll make sure I include that in my plan. And no matter what my plan is, you and Ivana will always be my most important clients."

Erin's multitasking skills had improved even more, which meant she could surf for prostitute survivor information while working on whatever Ava gave her. By the middle of the following week, she had found enough.

There are lots of sex trafficking victims rescue agencies around the globe. The UN Human Trafficking definition includes it. It's the recruitment, transportation, transfer, or harboring persons, by means of the threat, force leading to abduction, fraud, and deception, all intended to exploit the victim.

All the agencies or missions have survivor-led social justice-oriented programs that can heal victims first and then provide help for finding new careers.

I think I can put together what I'll call our Battered Demimonde Plan, but I better run this past Indira. And I'll do that after I have a peanut-buttered banana and Coke.

Indira's avatar showed even more patience-filled empathy than on Erin's last call, and her words showed it when she spoke after Erin finished.

"Your Battered Demimonde Plan has merit, and your idea for using the Deus Lab as a halfway house is reasonable. I will have Indy-M set it up. And regarding your security concerns, I will have Indy-M give you three encrypted cell phones containing tracking chips. You and your partners should use them only when discussing this project."

"I hadn't thought of that. What else have I missed?"

"Bring your partners with you the next time you visit. I will instruct Indy-M what injections all of you need for protection when looking for the ladies you wish to rescue. Other than that, you have everything covered. Please contact me when you have more to report."

"I will, and I thank you. Bye for now."

Alonzo had made little progress in finding at least one viable client who might give him a consulting project. He had postponed asking Monet for a recommendation for fear of mixing personal and professional worlds, but with the summer solstice having come and gone, he decided to visit at her embassy office, which would prevent his sisters from listening in to what he needed her to do. He knew that if he asked her at home, Eve's sharp ears would hear.

Monet's diplomatic sixth sense detected Alonzo's anxiety, so she let him talk as long as needed, which came after circling it for fifteen minutes.

"Do you remember much about that NAIA and IPWA work I was doing before Electra Kirchner disappeared? Weren't you going to work on the international angle?"

"Yes. She would become their de facto ambassador, and I would introduce her to appropriate leaders in Third World countries. Unfortunately, the momentum died when she vanished and will take too long to rebuild unless you have the resources."

Monet waited for him to react, but his blank expression told her to help him out.

"However, why not consider the NAIA piece? Perhaps Pequot Indian leader Feather Trueson or Connecticut Congressman Benjamin Chaska might want to push for a Native American Indian Alliance."

A glimmer of recognition came with his words.

"Thanks for reminding me. I had forgotten all about it. I'm going to tell Eve to check it out as soon as I get back to the office."

Brimming with newfound energy, Alonzo charged into their office two hours later but sat before blurting out,

"Monet just came up with a potential project that jibes with what you might remember about the NAIA. Does it?"

Eve reacted first.

"I really liked that catchy acronym. Electra had a way with words. But after twenty-some years, I'm not sure any of the people she was working with are still alive or still in politics."

Nila said,

"I think Nari and I were working in the LA office at the time. Do you have any DC names?"

"Congressman Benjamin Chaska from Connecticut. Whatcha think?"

The name sparked Eve to say,

"It's a possibility if he's still in politics. And if he's still a congressman, we can make a pitch to work on his re-election campaign by leveraging on the name Electra Kirhner."

"OK, you two give it a try. And while you're doing that, I'll rehearse for calling my last hope."

Alonzo called twice but no one answered, so he thought he would leave a callback message when placing the third, but Britt Starling answered. She must have forgotten his caller I.D. because her formal greeting omitted any personal touch.

"Hello, Commander Starling. This is Alonzo Cortez. We haven't talked for a long time. Did I catch you at a good time?"

"Now that's a name from the past. Yes. How are you?"

"That's why I'm calling, but before I explain, how are you and Boomer? Are NASA projects keeping you busy?"

"He left NASA five years ago to work for a DOD contractor. We talk a couple of times a year. I'm still with NASA, but they put me in a project consulting role."

"I hope both of you are keeping busy working on projects you like. And that's the reason I'm calling. My Strike Force Security business needs some contract work. Do you have any potential contacts?"

"That would depend on what you've been doing. I recall that you and Electra Kirchner helped us on control software as well as climate change Big Data analysis. She and some of her associates did the app development and analysis while you led some of the field projects. Are you still working with her?"

"Sorry to say, no. She departed for places unknown."

"That's too bad. What kind of projects could you handle?"

"Any project that has some sort of field expedition that needs a logistics and implementation coordinator. I'd be happy to lead as well as coordinate."

"I don't know of anything suitable at NASA, but I'll let Boomer know you called. He'll call you if he's interested. Why don't you Email your contact and Website info?"

"I will, and thanks for referring me to Boomer. So long."

Alonzo sat, thinking about his predicament after ending the call. It didn't take him long to decide that Erin Keenan's offer was looking better and better.

Unlike Alonzo, Ava and Ivana would choose an antonym of predicament when thinking about their current situation, and this morning, they weren't sitting. They were walking to the modeling department for her interview with one of the talent evaluators.

Ava gave final advice before tapping on the door to his private office.

"I'll introduce you, and then all you have to do is smile and follow his directions. Give me your purse so your hands are free. Maybe he'll let me stay."

Ivana's smile hadn't yet come out when Ricardo opened the door. Ava had never met him, but he looked bulkier and more imposing than she envisioned. He blocked the entrance and talked like a man who always took control.

"So, you are Ava Keenan from Pat's department, and this is your friend Ivana. How's her English?"

"It's getting better and better. She understands what people tell her much better than when she's telling them what she thinks. If you like, I can stay while you're interviewing her."

"No, that's OK. Just give me her resume and a video showing her in action. I'll take it from there. Depending on how it goes, she'll be done in an hour or two."

"Sounds good. I think you'll like her. Thanks for seeing her."

Ava shook his hand and then hugged Ivana before heading back to her office.

Ava had been there for twenty minutes when she realized she still had Ivana's purse.

I better go back and give it to her. She might need it when going to wherever Ricardo tells her.

While almost there, she noticed that all the other people working near his office occupied open cubicles, not closed-door spaces, but she didn't consider it further until she stood at the door.

What's going on in there? It sounds like some sort of commotion. Maybe she's changing into different clothes. I'll peek in to see what's going on.

One tiny look was all it took for her to see what had become a pain-filled predicament for Ivana. She was half-naked and pinned to the floor under Ricardo. One of his hands covered her mouth, while his pumping buttocks said another orifice was also under attack.

Ava whipped the pepper spray out of Ivana's purse before blasting the door open and screaming.

"Get off her, you brute."

Then she raced toward Ricardo, who had just enough time to swing his head in her direction. The pepper spray hit him right between the eyes, toppling him off. His screams filled the cubicles nearby, bringing workers followed by a security guard.

Ava didn't say a word, letting the scene speak for itself, until the security guard said,

"What's going on?"

Ricard yelled,

"This candidate is trying to blackmail me into hiring her. She ripped off her clothes and pulled me on top of her. And then her accomplice Ava Keenan, who works for Pat Peters, barges in and starts shooting pepper spray in my face. Get them outta here. You take'em to H.R. so they can fire Keenan."

"No. Everyone stay put. I'm calling Human Resources. They'll decide what to do."

An hour later, Ava decided that she and Ivana had been through enough for one day, so after helping rearrange Ivana's clothing, the two walked home. No words were needed. Ivana's hand in Ava's said it all.

"The Hunt for Demimonde Number One"

Ricardo bullied the H.R. Department into believing his story, using his seniority and reputation, along with similar modeling industry incidents to get Ava fired.

The episode discouraged Ivana from taking other modeling interviews, and the scuttlebutt surrounding Ava accompanied every interview she went on.

Erin tried to put a positive spin on the situation by coaching them toward new careers, and while she did that, Ivana and Ava asked her to help them launch their first demimonde rescue sortie. Ivana would pick a district to patrol at night, looking for one of her unfortunate Russian friends who had been brought to Manhattan. She dare not call them in advance for fear that her former john, Humpy, would discover her new identity, so on their patrols, Ivana would point, Ava and Erin would explain how they could help the friend, and then they would rush back to the car and drive off before the john found out she was missing.

Erin planned both the process of what they would do as well as the protocol of the how, which included wearing the right clothes, concealing self-defense weapons in purses, and memorizing what to say. They actually role-played before taking the first couple of rehearsal drive-throughs, which were meant to reconnoiter districts. No one left the car, and they learned the art of remaining in the shadows.

Erin could tell that Ava and Renee had become bored by doing nothing other than role-playing and reconnoitering, so when the August weather cleared during the last week of the month, she picked the first sortie to start after dark on Friday, a day and time Ivana knew would have plenty of streetwalkers and guys driving around looking for tricks. Erin's rental car would blend right in with the traffic.

Ivana knew what to look for, and she practiced spotting the johns while looking for her unfortunate cohorts. And she kept her team informed of her intentions. At a little past midnight, she gave the go signal. Erin parked just far enough from the streetwalker's corner to be inconspicuous. Then she and Ava made first contact.

Erin pulled some bills out of her purse to get the Russian hooker's attention before saying,

"If you're from Russia, we have a retired streetwalker friend who wants to help you break the habit. Whether or not you come with us right now, you can keep the money."

"I can't walk away. I need the money, and if my john finds out, he beat me."

"Erin said,

"Our friend's gone through the same and worse. Look, we can't stand here. Come with us, and you can decide for yourself. You'll be no worse off than you are right now."

Erin's words worked. Ava locked arms with the hooker, and Erin led them toward the car. But no sooner had she taken the second step when the john came out of nowhere and tackled her. Then he punched Ava enough times to put her on top of Erin. The poor hooker was about to suffer the same punishment, but two gunshots split the night, bringing the john down. Ivanna had come to the rescue.

She picked up her counterpart and must have said the right Russian words because both ran to the car. Erin picked up Ava, and they followed fast enough to climb in and drive away with lights out and Demimonde number one in the back seat, sobbing in Ivanna's arms.

No words were needed on the drive back to the condominium. Everyone said silent prayers, giving thanks for surviving. There would be plenty of time tomorrow to say more.

Chapter 14
September 2194

"The Return of Bigger Brother"

Ava and Ivana had already decided how best to settle their first rescue lady for the first night in their condo. Erin thought Maria looked like a shorter version of Ivana, though not as pretty and much older. Years of living a damaging and dangerous lifestyle had taken its toll.

Ivana took charge of cleaning her up. Two hours later, the foursome sat ready to talk in the living room, Ivana on the sofa with Maria seemingly joined at her hip and the other two in chairs near either end.

Erin could see in Ivana's demeanor that tonight had been a transcendent moment, so Erin looked at her when saying,

"We're lucky for the gun, but I must ask, how did you get it?"

"I figure out using Deep-Dark Web."

"Please show Ava how to get there. You two should decide what else to get to help Maria. Is she hooked on cocaine?"

"Yes. I will unhook her. She been here longer and uses English better, but I will teach her more better words."

"OK, and let me outline our collective next steps. Ivana works each day helping Maria. You two meet daily with Ava. Meanwhile, Ava will continue finding new careers and job interviews for all of you, and when you are ready, we'll go to the Deus Lab so you see how it fits into our rescue program. Now, let's get a good night's sleep so we can get to work tomorrow."

In the following weeks, everyone did so by following Erin's grand plan, but not even Erin knew that Zoltan Sultani's snoopers had been observing her, thanks to a consulting business plant. If she had ever traced through Zoltan's connection to the old Electra and Alonzo, she might have known what to look out for, but she didn't have a clue, and if Alonzo did, he would have alerted his sisters. Too bad he didn't.

Eve's political instincts and people skills had landed a campaign consulting assignment with Congressman Chaska. The sisters sat in Alonzo's office, Eve explaining what they would do this week, October's first.

"There's an all-parties press conference being held at noon Wednesday on the steps of the Capitol. All the presidential candidates agree that the public's top concerns are protecting the border, the economy, and national security in that order. I wanna hear how the candidates' promises differ."

"I like that, so keep at it. And call me on your cell if something's gonna break."

"We will, and don't forget to keep a 24-7 broadcast playing in the background. You've said a bunch of times that your previous mentor told you it's a great way to stay in constant contact with what's going on."

Nila added,

"Have you and Monet lined up anything for your IPWA contract?"

"She's getting close enough to bring me into her meetings. If we're lucky, we'll get it signed right after the election."

Eve said,

"Well, we have our marching orders, so let's keep moving."

Alonzo stopped daydreaming long enough Wednesday morning to wish his sisters good luck before returning to brooding.

Too bad Electra never came back. She had a knack for finding connections no one else saw, which always put us back in action. Well, maybe something'll come up that'll do the same for me.

Eve weaved through the crowd flowing from the foot of the Capitol's stairs, towing Nila. They got close enough to the speaker's podium to catch all the nuances in body language, which both sisters knew politicians had mastered, and they liked to compare and contrast when each speaker finished to keep boredom from taking over.

The fourth speaker had just started when a wave of crowd buzzing interrupted. Eve looked around to see the cause but saw nothing until shouts came from the back.

"What the?... SUVs coming our way...They're gonna plow into us...Run..."

The sisters ran with the crowd until a tremendous blast brought everyone around them down.

The theme music that always preceded news bulletins brought Alonzo out of his musing.

"This just in. A three-SUV suicide caravan just blew up the noon press conference being held on the steps of Washington's Capitol Building. That's all we know at this minute because we have lost contact with our onsite crew. We are rushing a replacement to give you video ASAP, but until then you might want to listen to what our experts have to say. Could this be the work of that long-rumored 'Bigger Brother' conspiracy? Have they returned? Please stay tuned for what our experts are telling us."

Alonzo clicked off the broadcast and called Eve. Getting no answer, he tried Nila. No luck there either, so he rushed out to see for himself what might become a catastrophe in both his personal as well as professional worlds.

He waited for hours with others who had jammed the area, hoping for any news as soon as the Department of Homeland Security and sister agencies were organized. Dusk had come by the time he got to talk with one of the officials manning the Crisis Support Center.

He showed several I.D.'s before saying,

"I'm Alonzo Cortez. I have a DC consulting business, and two of my employees, Eve Cortez and Nila Bose, were covering the conference. Do you have them on any of your lists?"

"Wait, please. I'll check."

The official spoke via cellphone to someone who transferred the call. Alonzo's anxiety grew the longer he waited. By the time the official spoke to him, Alonzo could read a bad outcome in his expression and voice.

"Please go to the Victims Tent for further instructions."

Alonzo followed orders, doing his best to stifle emotions.

Chapter 15
October 2194

"Over and Out"

Alonzo's worst fears had materialized, but his Navy SEAL experience had exposed him to events that were almost as catastrophic, so he dealt with the deaths of Nari and Eve, relying only on Monet and Erin for consoling thoughts. He went back to work one day after the closed-casket private funeral.

Alonzo tried to keep busy, but lack of clients made that difficult, so a couple of weeks later, he called his boss. Erin answered on the third ring, using a personal greeting after recognizing the caller's I.D. that had shown up on her cellphone.

"Hello, Alonzo. I imagine you're still working through the loss of your sisters. How are you feeling?"

"Better than a couple of weeks ago. I'm trying to fill in for Eve and Nari on the Chaska campaign, but they were better than me. Anyway, I'm calling to remind you about what Electra Kirchner taught me. Always look for connections to whatever events hit you, no matter how weird they seem."

"Maybe we can talk about it the next time we get together. Now that you work for me, do you think your events and mine might be connected?"

"Anything's possible, so just keep paying attention."

"I will. Anything else."

"Nope, I'll just say 'Over and Out' until we get together again."

Erin filed his recommendation for further consideration sometime after her next big event: another Demimonde sortie that would be a go late this coming Saturday night, only two days away. She would let Ava and Ivana practice alone. They already knew what to wear, how to talk, and what to bring.

On Saturday morning, Erin rented a typically boring sedan and practiced driving while memorizing the routes leading to and from the cruising zones. As the trio drove away that night, she tried to keep the mood light by playing the radio, but she turned it off when they approached the danger zone.

"Pay attention to anything suspicious going on."

Ava asked,

"Like what?"

"As far as we know, nobody's detected us, but that could change. Be on the lookout for cars or something following us."

"OK. Ivana, what else?"

"Maybe couple a pimps shooting at us. If so, we no stop. We drive away."

The weather forecast might have been the reason for lighter-than-normal traffic. The threat of lightning and thunder frightens everyone, no matter their intentions.

Even Erin had become bored by the lack of possible action and was about to end their patrol when, out of nowhere from behind, an SUV cut them off. Erin swerved to the left, hitting the curb and coming to a dead stop. The SUV stopped on the same side, only four car lengths ahead, and when a big man sprang out from the passenger side, Erin floored the accelerator while swerving back to the right.

But rattled nerves made her misjudge the spacing. She smashed into the big man, pinning him to his open door before ripping it off.

Ava screamed after twisting to see out the rear.

"My god, he looks dead."

Erin said nothing until slamming on the brakes after ducking down a street several blocks ahead.

"You two, get out and run to a subway station. I'll keep driving until I know I'm in the clear. Now go. I'll call when I know I'm safe."

Erin kept crisscrossing streets, hoping to elude any pursuers, but headlights crisscrossing whenever she did replaced her hope with mounting fear. As the gap relentlessly shrank, she knew she couldn't outrun the pursuer. And she realized a deadly mistake a second too late.

Erin had careened onto a West Side Parkway entrance ramp, taking her to an elevated two-lane divided section. She had no way out.

She could do nothing but floor the accelerator, hoping that something would happen to put the odds of survival in her favor. But the car couldn't handle the speed on the now rain-slick road. Try as she might, Erin couldn't control the steering wheel.

She drove over the divider, which pitched the car against the opposite barrier. It bounced off and then drove over the divider again. The momentum then sent the front end skyward toward the guardrail.

Leaping over the guardrail, the bottom of the car barely ticked it, hardly altering the parabolic trajectory that would soon reach an apex before accelerating Erin on a descending arc into the unknown waters of the Hudson River, now out of sight, shrouded in the darkness below that lightning flashes couldn't penetrate.

An eerie silence was Erin's only companion in the car, but an exceptional jolt that she had never felt until this moment vibrated every neural fiber in her brain, bringing with it awe-filled words.

I HAVE FINALLY RETURNED ... I AM ELECTRA ... BUT I AM MORE ... I AM ALSO ERIN AND ALISHA ... AND I NOW REMEMBER ALL THOSE WHO HAVE COME BEFORE ... THEY ARE PART OF ME TOO FROM LONG, LONG AGO.

BUT FOR HOW LONG MAY I STAY?... IT IS NOT MINE TO SAY... FOR THE ANSWER IS BEYOND MY CONTROL...

AND I FINALLY FEEL A CONSOLING INNER PEACE...

I SAY WITH FINAL THANKSGIVING,
TO WHATEVER GODS MAY BE.
THAT NO LIFE LIVES FOREVER,
THAT DEAD MEN RISE UP NEVER,
THAT EVEN THE WEARIEST RIVER,
WINDS SOMEWHERE SAFE TO SEA.

THE END